CYNTHIA HICKEY

Christmas Stalker
Misty Hollow, Book 8

Cynthia Hickey

Copyright © **2022 Cynthia Hickey**
Published by: Winged Publications

    This book is a work of fiction. Names, characters, places, and incidents are the product of the author's imagination and are used fictitiously. Any resemblance to actual events, locales, or persons, living or dead, is coincidental.

No part of this book may be copied or distributed without the author's consent.

All rights reserved.

ISBN-13: 978-1-956654-86-8

Merry Christmas. May yours be only stalked by love and Joy..

Chapter One

He spotted her the instant he stepped through the doors of the hotel's ballroom. Hair the color of the coffee he drank every morning, a dress the color of the wine he enjoyed every evening. Sitting next to a frumpy blonde, the vision in the corner was the missing piece in his life. His middle. He had to have her.

She frowned at something her friend said, her brows lowering over eyes the color of bluebells. He truly had never seen anything lovelier. Not wanting to make her acquaintance yet, he stayed on the outskirts of the party he crashed. A Christmas party full of people in fancy clothes and fake smiles.

Taking his time, blending in with his dark suit and Christmas-green tie, he headed for the buffet. His stomach rumbled at the sight of carved roast beef. He hadn't eaten since that morning and only a bagel then. Handing out justice took all his time.

He filled his plate and searched for a table where he could view the pretty woman but not attract her attention. Not yet, at least. He had to know whether her prettiness went deep inside or merely flashed on the surface.

After finding out the woman he'd once loved had been spending time with his friend, well...he moved with a little more caution now. The good thing about being cheated on? He smiled. He now knew his life's purpose. Rid the world of cheats and liars.

~

Brynlee Bourge balanced a plate of food in one hand and a flute of Champagne in the other. "Since you forced me to come to this party with you, can we at least sit down to eat?" She glared at her friend, Madison Wells.

"I'm trying to find someone handsome enough to warrant conversation." She grinned. "Stop being such a fuddy-duddy, Brynn."

"Librarians are supposed to be fuddy-duddies." Not waiting any longer for her friend, she marched to the nearest table and sat across from an older couple who held hands under the starched white tablecloth. So cute. "Merry Christmas, Mr. and Mrs. Anderson."

"Merry Christmas, Brynlee. I didn't know you were a member of the country club?" Mrs. Anderson took a sip of water from the crystal goblet next to her plate.

"I'm not. I came with my friend, Maddy." Who, at the moment, was giggling at something one of the servers said.

"Ah, yes. The Wells family are huge contributors to the arts." She set her glass down with precision, matching the sweat marks on the tablecloths. "It's only fitting the two of you be here since this dinner is to raise money for the library addition."

Firmly put in her place, Brynn ducked her head

and focused on her food as if she was starved. She fought back a sigh. It was her place to be there as head librarian, but for an introvert, social gatherings of this size were torture. All she wanted to do was spend her days helping readers find books and her evenings with her nose buried in the latest mystery or suspense.

Fiction helped erase the danger she'd escaped from a few years ago, similar but Fiction's happy endings gave her hope she'd one day escape the memories of her assault. Her hand trembled as she reached for the Champagne flute and downed the last swallow before reaching for her water glass.

Movement to her right caught her eye. A dark-haired man in a suit sitting at a table in the corner seemed to be watching her. With his face shadowed by a large silk plant, she couldn't make out his features. Why were parties so dark?

A server approached with another flute. "Compliments of the gentleman in the corner." She set it in front of Brynn and moved on.

"Oh, a secret admirer." Mrs. Anderson clasped her hands together. "How sweet."

Brynn pushed the flute aside. "One's my limit, I'm afraid." She cut the man another glance. He raised his flute in a toast.

Although she couldn't see his eyes, she felt as if they bored through her. She shuddered and pushed to her feet. "Excuse me." She rushed from the room and into the atrium in search of the women's restroom. Veering left, she ducked into the restroom, slamming the door of the stall behind her. Brynn had learned two years ago to trust her instincts, and they were telling her the mystery man wasn't someone who wanted to be her friend.

Sitting on the toilet seat, she buried her face in her hands and took deep breaths. One, two...

The door opened. "Brynn?" Maddy's voice drifted under the stall. "Are you okay? I saw you rush from the room. Are you sick?"

"No, I'm fine. Just overwhelmed."

"Come on out. Let's refresh our lipstick."

Maddy's solution for everything. A fresh coat of a brightly colored lipstick.

The door opened again.

"An employee delivered a note," Maddy said. "It's labeled to the woman in the wine-colored dress. Since I'm wearing green, it has to be you."

Brynn's heart leaped into her throat, and she stepped from the stall. Her hand trembled as she took the note and opened it. "Your beauty, your kindness, your sweet shyness. All this makes me want you. You are mine."

"Creepy." Maddy peered over her shoulder. "It was sweet until the last line. Who sent it?"

"No idea." Other than that it had to be the man who sent her the Champagne. "I'm going home."

"Okay. I'll drive you." Disappointment laced her friend's words.

"Absolutely not. Stay. Have fun. I'll call for a ride. See you tomorrow at work." Brynn dropped the note into the trash and yanked the door open, almost expecting to see the stranger standing there. With the coast clear, she raced for the concierge's desk and asked him to call her a ride.

She rubbed her hands up and down her arms against a sudden chill and stared at the front doors. Her mouth dried at the reflection of a tall man in a dark suit watching her from the entrance to the ballroom. No time to wait for her ride. She had to go now. Lifting her dress to her ankles, she whirled and raced out a side door, making a beeline for the brightly lit park close by. Even with night having fallen, people strolled the path that wound between trees lit up with lights. Wreaths adorned old-fashioned lampposts. Her rented home waited on the other side of the park. Her beacon.

A glance over her shoulder showed the man following, his dark suit a speck against the purity of a freshly fallen snow. With a gasp, she increased her speed. Another glance showed the man heading in the opposite direction as he tugged at his tie.

Brynn ducked behind a tree to catch her breath. When she peeked around, he'd discarded his suit jacket. Was the man undressing? She closed her eyes, said a quick prayer for safety, then peeked again. No sight of him. Her heart rate slowed.

Lifting her dress again, she resumed her mad dash toward home. She careened around a corner and smashed into a man in a white long-sleeved shirt and dark pants.

"Whoa." He reached out to steady her.

She screamed and jumped back. "Leave me alone or I'll scream again."

~

"I'm sorry I frightened you." Weston Hoover reached for her again.

The woman shrank back.

"Are you okay? Do you need help?"

She shook her head hard enough that her hair obscured her features. "Leave me alone." The woman made a wide berth around him and resumed her dash through the park.

Weston studied the grounds in the direction from which she'd come. Clearly distraught, she'd acted frightened, but he didn't see anyone who appeared to be following her. Wanting to make sure she made it to her destination safely, he turned in the direction she'd fled.

The color of her dress made it easy for him to catch sight of her ahead. She'd slowed to a fast walk, her hands rubbing her arms against the winter chill. Why was she outside without a coat?

Weston knew why he was. He'd worked late at the diner. Not having taken a coat to begin with, he now had to jog home in an effort to stay warm.

The woman glanced back, her eyes widening at the sight of him. She darted forward again, leaving the path and heading for a group of teenagers hanging out under a bridge. Not the safest place to seek safety. Then she pointed his way. The boys turned toward him. She sprinted in the opposite direction.

"Hey, dude, you bothering this lady?" One of them wearing a football letter jacket crossed his arms. The pungent smell of marijuana wafted from the fabric.

"No." Weston heaved a sigh. "She's obviously frightened about something. I'm following her to make sure she makes it to her destination safely."

"She said you've been following her since leaving the hotel." The teen jerked his chin toward the newly erected Misty Hollow Regency built by a mob boss the year before he arrived in town, at least that's what someone had told him. The place marred the landscape of the small town. A miserable ploy to bring tourists to their town. Since it worked, no one proposed tearing it down.

"Nope. She collided into me. I'm simply playing Good Samaritan." He crossed his arms to match the boy's stance as the woman disappeared from sight. "Thanks to you, she's now gone with no one watching out for her."

"That's Miss Bourge, the librarian. If you were from around here, you'd know that."

"I'm new to town. Just arrived last week."

"Turn around, Mister, or we'll pound you. Come on, boys." He turned and marched back to the bridge.

Since he had no idea where the woman would have gone, Weston resumed his jog home. He'd stop by the library on his break the next day and explain to the woman that he hadn't meant her any harm.

Someone or something had definitely frightened her enough to send her out into the cold, snowy night alone without the proper clothing. He glanced around again.

The dark form of a man stood under a streetlamp seeming to stare in the direction the woman had gone.

Chapter Two

Brynn closed the romantic suspense she'd just finished, left it on the table to put away later, and dashed out the door, her mind already on the next book she wanted to read. If she didn't hurry to the diner, she wouldn't have time to eat before opening the library.

Being Saturday, almost every booth and stool was full. A decorated Christmas tree filled one corner of the room. Garlands hung from the lunch counter, and Christmas carols played on the radio.

She followed the hostess who wore bells on her ears to a small table near the kitchen. "Biscuits and chocolate gravy, please." She smiled and took an unread book from her purse.

The cover depicted a woman running through the snow. The similarity between what she saw and what she'd endured the night before tempted her to slip the book back into her purse. No, she'd started reading suspense novels for a reason—to conquer her fear, to see justice done. She wouldn't become a fraidy cat because of a chase through the park. Maybe the man hadn't meant any harm.

She was pretty, or so people told her. Why wouldn't a man pay her attention? Brynn glanced around the diner. Familiar faces smiled and waved. Warmth filled her. She was surrounded by people who cared for her. Perhaps she'd overreacted the night before.

A server set two large biscuits and a bowl of chocolate gravy in front of her. Brynn thanked her, reminded the girl she had an overdue library book, and opened the book in her hand to read as she ate.

The gravy seemed thicker and richer than before, the biscuits a bit more flaky. Brynn closed her eyes at the silkiness of the chocolate.

Someone put a hand on her shoulder. "I'll tell the new chef you like his biscuits."

She opened her eyes and stared into the face of the diner's owner, Lucy. "They're fabulous."

"Wait until you see him. Talk about eye candy." She wiggled her eyebrows. "I'll send him out to say hello in a minute."

Brynn nodded and returned to her breakfast. The diner had never lacked for business as far as she knew, but once word spread that the new chef was even better than Chef Rawlings had been, they'd have to start taking reservations.

One glance at the clock sent her to her feet. She tossed money on the table. "I'll meet him at lunch," she told Lucy on her way out.

Her feet pounded the pavement as she raced toward the library down the street. She owned an older model car but only drove when it rained. Everything she needed was within walking distance, or running distance in this case.

One gray-haired woman waited outside, stomping her feet against the cold sidewalk. She glanced at her watch as Brynn arrived. "Two minutes to spare."

"Your watch is fast, Mrs. Washington." She flashed a grin and unlocked the door, stepping aside to let the other woman enter first. "Do you want me to carry your books?" The woman had about five in her bag from the size of it.

"I carried them this far, thank you." She bustled inside, set her books on the return shelf, and made a beeline for the new releases.

Brynn chuckled and headed for her desk. She had an hour before children would arrive for story time, a highlight of her week.

The busy morning sped by. At noon, she locked up the library for the next hour and hurried back to the diner. Today's special was potato soup, and she couldn't wait to see how well the new chef did with an old favorite.

A man stepped from the bank and into her path. She collided with him, spun, tossed a quick apology, and resumed her pace. Ten minutes to the diner and back left little time to dally. She burst into the diner like a gale-force wind and waited to be seated.

~

Where was his love going in such a hurry? He'd caught a whiff of her floral perfume when she'd ran into him and reached out to touch her. Unfortunately, his fingers had done nothing more than brush across the sleeve of her coat before she'd sprinted away like a gazelle.

He watched her back until she entered the diner, almost wishing he'd followed her. Instead, he turned toward her house. His task for the day was to enter her world, get to know her a little better, before they met face-to-face. If he knew what she liked, he'd know exactly how to woo her.

After making sure no one paid him any attention, he picked the lock on the door to the mid-century-style house, grateful for the tall hedge on each side that gave the place privacy. He'd have to talk to her about those hedges one day. A woman alone shouldn't have a place that gave predators easy access.

Inside, he closed the door behind him and took a deep breath. Her perfume lingered like a mist. A bookcase filled one entire wall of the living room. A brown sofa covered with a colorful afghan, an easy chair, and a trunk used as a coffee table were the only other furniture.

Through an arch, he spotted a table with four chairs and a modest kitchen just beyond that. Down a short hall were two bedrooms, one with a desk and laptop, and a bathroom. She lived modestly. He smiled and stepped in front of the bookcase.

Ah, so she preferred mystery and suspense. He frowned at the many covers with a man on them, then flipped through hoping she wasn't the type to like books full of sex. She didn't appear to be. Some of the tension left his shoulders. He turned and picked up the book on the coffee table.

After reading the blurb on the back, he flipped through the pages reading random passages before setting the book down. Now he knew exactly how to win over his sweetheart. He picked up a stack of mail and read her name, Brynlee Bourge.

All he needed to do now was find his own copy of the book she'd been reading. Then, he'd put his plan into action.

"She's at the table to your right as you exit the kitchen." Lucy hung an order for him. "Brynn said she hopes the soup is as good as the prior chef's."

Weston laughed. "I'll be sure to ask her myself whether it meets her approval."

After breakfast, Lucy had gone on and on about how much Miss Bourge enjoyed his chocolate gravy and biscuits. He'd make sure to add a roll to her order of soup. Maybe he'd deliver her order himself. It was time to start meeting the residents of Misty Hollow, and he might as well start with the woman Lucy seemed so fond of.

He ladled the soup into a bowl and set a roll on a plate. As he exited the kitchen he froze. Miss Bourge was the woman who had run from him the night before.

Seeing him, she jumped to her feet. Her eyes rolled back, and she crumpled to the floor before he could react. He set the food on the table and knelt beside her. "Ma'am? Miss Bourge?"

"What happened?" Lucy shoved him out of the way.

"It's a long—"

Her eyes fluttered open, and she scooted away from him. "Leave me alone."

"What is going on, Brynlee?" Lucy glanced from her to him. "Weston?"

"He chased me through the park last night." The wall stopped her retreat.

"No." He shook his head, glancing at the stern and shocked faces around him. "I wanted to help."

"I've called the sheriff," someone called out. "No one messes with our librarian."

He heaved a sigh and stood, only to find himself shoved into a booth. "Listen to me. I'm telling you I didn't chase her. There was someone else out there." Weston tried to explain about the man he'd spotted under the streetlamp.

"Keep it for the sheriff," someone from a corner booth yelled.

Lucy helped Brynlee onto a chair and shot him a glare. "You'd better be able to explain yourself or you'll find yourself without a job."

"I'm trying to. Miss Bourge—"

Lucy shook her head. "I agree with the others. Wait for the sheriff."

Which took about ten minutes. Sheriff Westbrook approached the booth where Weston sat, then motioned for both him and Brynlee to follow him to the diner's office. "Go about your business, folks. I've got this." He motioned for Lucy to remain in the main part of the diner.

In the office, he perched on the corner of the desk. "Sit." He waved at the two chairs in the room. "Brynlee, you go first." He crossed his arms.

"This man stalked me last night." The color had returned to her face. Instead of frightened, she now looked irate.

Good. Weston didn't think he could convince the sheriff to believe him if she still looked as if she'd keel over if he glanced at her. "I did not. She ran into me looking as if the devil himself were after her. For some insane reason, she got the idea I was chasing her."

"You sent me Champagne and a note at the Christmas party, then followed me from the hotel."

"Sheriff, I didn't go to a Christmas party last night.

I was working here…"

"Yes, you were. I saw you right outside the building. You shed your clothes before I ran into you," she said.

The sheriff's brow furrowed. "Hold on, Brynlee. Mr. Hoover, what were you wearing?"

"Call me Weston. I wore black slacks and a long-sleeved white shirt."

"So did my stalker! I saw him remove his tie and jacket."

"Would you swear in a court of law that Mr…Weston was the man after you?"

Her shoulders slumped. "No. I never got a good look at his face during the party. But why would a man be out in the park in the cold without proper clothing?"

"You were," Weston pointed out.

"Because I was running from you." She crossed her arms and narrowed her eyes.

"Were you at the party alone?" The sheriff tilted his head. "My wife and I were there, but I didn't see you."

"I didn't stay long, but I went with my friend Madison Wells. She stayed after I left."

He turned to Weston. "Tell me about the man you say you saw."

"After a group of high-school football players confronted me about bothering Brynlee—" he shot a look her way to see whether she objected to him using her first name. When she didn't react, he continued. "She ran down the pathway under a bridge. I lost sight of her and turned to head home. That's when I saw the man. The light was behind him, so I couldn't see his face. He was clearly watching her."

"If you couldn't see his face, then you can't tell with any certainty which way he looked." Sheriff Westbrook straightened. "It appears we simply have a misunderstanding here. Mr. Hoover is not a threat to you, Brynlee. I did a background check on him when Lucy hired him."

Did he do that for everyone? He pushed to his feet. "If we're done here, I've a diner full of guests wanting their food. I'll heat up your soup, Brynlee, and put it in a to-go container." Without waiting for a thank you from her or a reply from the sheriff, he marched from the office. Ignoring the glares of the diners, he went back to the sanctuary of the kitchen, fixed Brynlee's lunch to-go, and handed it to Lucy. "Let's forget this day ever happened."

"I'm sorry, but we're pretty protective of our people," she said. "No offense."

"Forget it." He glanced over as Brynlee stood in the doorway.

"Do you promise it wasn't you?"

"Yep." He turned away.

"Then, I'm happy to tell you that even cold, that's the best potato soup I've ever had."

When he turned around, she had gone.

"See? We're good people." Lucy grinned. "All it takes is a little time to get to know you. Her liking your soup will be a giant step toward the town accepting you."

What they needed to be worried about was the man in the park instead of accusing him of harassing a woman which was something he would never do.

Chapter Three

He read the first chapter of the book he'd checked out of the library, wanting to get every detail right. The sight of Brynlee's face—he knew her name now from her nametag—kept hiding the words on the page. She'd smiled up at him and told him what a good book he was about to read. The book still held the warmth of her touch. Unfortunately, he'd had to use his alias of David Brown to check out a library card. He couldn't have her knowing his true identity. Not yet.

In the book, the antagonist cut the brake lines on the hero's truck. Who was the hero in Brynlee's story? Someday it would be him, but as of now....He closed the book and drummed his fingers on the cover. Only one man came to mind. The one who had tried to follow Brynlee in the park. The chef of Lucy's Diner.

A quick glance at the clock alerted him to the passing of time. He knew where the chef lived, and if he hurried, he'd be able to get the job done before the man left for work.

He rushed from the room he rented at the hotel and into the parking garage. His Mercedes's trunk held the necessary tools. 'David' was always prepared for anything.

Ten minutes later, he slid under a Ford F-150 and cut the brake line. There weren't any dangerous curves between the man's house and the diner, but hopefully the danger would be great enough to attract attention. Because he really wanted to attract Brynlee's attention.

Job complete, he wiped his hands on a clean rag and hurried back to his car. All he could do now was read another chapter of the book and wait. Maybe grab a bite of breakfast at the diner as his love did every morning.

He returned to his room, showered, put contacts in his eyes, then strolled across the park and into the diner. Brynlee sat at the same table she sat at every meal. She really needed to learn to cook. Something he'd remedy once they were together.

He smiled at the pretty young hostess and followed her to another small table wishing very much that he could approach Brynlee and ask to sit with her. Through the kitchen window, he spotted the chef. No accident yet. It would have been better to sabotage the diner, but it wasn't in the book.

After perusing the menu, he ordered a ham-and-cheese omelet, then opened his book. He smiled to himself at the sight of Brynlee doing the same only with a different story in hand. Someday, they'd sit side by side and read together if she desired. It did surprise him that she enjoyed suspense novels rather than something sweeter. Did she have a dark side he didn't know about? She was becoming a little more interesting with each passing day.

~

Brynlee finished her breakfast of strawberry crepes, paid her bill, then tapped on the door leading to the kitchen. Mortification filled her every time she thought of the fiasco yesterday.

Weston turned from the stove. "What's up?"

"I really am sorry. Both for accusing you and for fainting. I'm not that kind of girl. You know, one without a backbone. I hadn't eaten, my blood sugar was low, and seeing you...well, it shocked me."

"No worries." He flashed a quick grin. "I don't hold grudges."

She tilted her head. His words sounded nice, but the guarded look in his eyes said he wasn't as fine as he said. She'd noticed a few of the other diners' cold shoulders toward him. "They'll warm up to you. Really, they will. Why don't you join me for supper tonight? If folks see us out and about together, they'll forget all about yesterday."

His brows drew together over eyes the color of dark chocolate. "What time do you get off work?"

"Five o'clock." She smiled. "See you then." She knew just the place to go so they'd be seen by a lot of the town's residents. Lucy's was the number-one spot, but the Mexican-food restaurant was a close second. Maybe she'd take him up the mountain. As busy as he was cooking for Lucy, he probably hadn't seen the town lights at night as they glimmered through the trees.

At five o'clock on the dot, she locked the library and turned to greet Weston as he pulled to the curb. "Punctual. I like that."

He slid out and opened the passenger door for her. "Lucy seemed overly thrilled to take over the cooking so we could go out. She wouldn't be playing matchmaker, would she?" His eyes twinkled under the streetlamp.

"Most likely." Brynn returned his smile. "I'll set

her straight in the morning." She slid into the truck and directed him toward the restaurant.

"I'm kind of surprised you invited me out," he said, climbing in the driver's seat. "You give me the impression of being...reserved."

She shrugged. "I am, but I also make right when I've done something wrong. I'll persuade the townspeople to trust you if it's the last thing I do."

"Sounds menacing." He chuckled and pulled away from the curb. "I know that time will turn them around. Any more feelings of being followed?"

"No, thank goodness. I'm starting to think I panicked and imagined the whole thing. I don't do well with crowds, and that Christmas party was full of people."

"Good." He smiled. "I'd hate to think of you in danger. Promise me that if you ever feel that way again, you'll call me."

"I don't have your number."

"You will before the night is through." He pulled into the parking lot of the restaurant.

She'd never had someone seem to care so much about her welfare. Brynn kind of liked it and studied him with fresh new eyes. Maybe it wouldn't hurt to form a friendship with the town's new chef. Other than Maddy, she didn't have many friends. Oh, the townspeople were all friendly enough, but she didn't visit with any of them on a regular basis.

~

Weston wouldn't argue, but he still didn't understand Brynlee's determination to make things right. Wouldn't her telling the people of Misty Hollow she'd been mistaken be enough? Or was she lonely enough to shove aside her solitude to spend time with him?

Either way, there were worse things than having supper with a gorgeous woman. He browsed the menu, choosing enchiladas with Spanish rice. He laughed when Brynlee ordered the same. "Healthy appetite."

"It helps that I walk everywhere unless it's snowing or raining." She handed their server the menus. "What brought you to Misty Hollow?"

"The opening for a chef at the diner. I worked in Little Rock, but the pace was too much for me. I wanted the small-town life, and Lucy said she'd split the cooking with me. I still think she needs to hire another chef, but that's up to her. How long have you lived here?"

"All my life."

Which explained the town's protectiveness over her. "Any family?"

"Parents, but they're living the dream and traveling Europe." She took a sip of the ice water set in front of her and dipped a nacho chip into a bowl of salsa. "I talk to them when they're somewhere with good cell service. If you aren't busy after we eat, we could go up to the lookout. Have you been?"

"Will I see the mist everyone talks about?"

"No, you'd have to go in the morning for that."

"Good. Another date." He grinned, enjoying the way pink rose to her cheeks. "I'd love to go to the lookout with you. When I was a teenager, that's something I'd say to a pretty girl to convince her to go parking."

"Oh." Her eyes widened. "No, I, uh—"

"I'm teasing, Brynlee." He straightened as their

food was set in front of them.

As they ate, she told him to call her Brynn and filled him in on all the small-town gossip, including what seemed like a lot of crime over the last year or so. She didn't seem bothered by any of it, chatting as if the mob trying to move in was an everyday occurrence.

He refused to let her pay for her meal, and with his hand on the small of her back, he guided her back to the truck. The temperature had dropped by several degrees as the sun lowered in the sky, prompting him to turn up the heater in the truck. "You sure you want to go up the mountain with it being this cold."

"I'm wearing a wool coat. I'll be fine. Will you?" She arched a brow as if daring him.

His mouth twitched. "I can handle the cold, sweetheart. Buckle up." As he drove, he noticed the brake pedal pressing farther toward the floor each time he used it. Great. One more expense he didn't need.

"There." Brynn pointed to a clearing on the side of the road.

He parked and jogged around the truck to let her out. This high up the mountain, a frigid wind blew, dropping the temperature further. He put an arm around her shoulders to keep him warm as much as her.

A railing stood between them and a deep drop-off. Lights from the buildings in the valley twinkled like Christmas lights. "It really is pretty."

She nodded. "Looks this way every night of the year, even in the rain. Then, the lights are blurred a bit, but still beautiful."

He cast a sideways look at her. The moon cast her skin with an unearthly glow and painted a silver halo on her dark hair. All she needed were wings to complete the heavenly look. An overwhelming urge to kiss her overcame him, and he took a step away from her.

They stood that way for maybe ten minutes before Brynn shivered as a light rain started to fall. "I guess it really is too cold. Especially with the threat of sleet."

"Thank goodness." He guided her back to the truck and cranked up the heater. "My jacket isn't as warm as I thought."

"Everything not covered by my coat was freezing." She smiled and clicked her seatbelt into place. "Thank you for coming with me."

"Thanks for inviting me." He turned the vehicle around and headed back the way they'd come.

The mountain switchbacks had him driving below the speed limit. Weston didn't need the road to ice over and send them sliding over the edge. He tapped the brake while going around a sharp curve.

The pedal went all the way to the floor. His breath hitched and he cast a quick look at Brynn. "Hold on."

"Why?" Her eyes widened, and she gripped the handle to the right of her head.

"Because we don't have any brakes."

Chapter Four

Brynn's blood turned to ice as her grip on the handle above her head tightened. "What do you mean we don't have any brakes?"

"They aren't working." His knuckles whitened on the steering wheel. "Don't worry. I got this."

"You aren't a race car driver!"

"No, but I was a rambunctious teenager. I had a souped-up Mustang and led the cops on a lot of crazy chases over curvy mountain roads."

Was he insane? "That was a long time ago." What if he'd lost the skill? She let out a squeak as they rounded a curve at a speed too high to be safe.

"Let me concentrate on the road. No squeaky sounds, please."

The truck lifted on two tires going around another curve, then dropped with a teeth-shattering thump to all four. Brynn closed her eyes and prayed like she'd never prayed before.

"I'll pull over at the first available spot." Weston leaned forward to peer through an increasing downpour.

Brynn knew this road. There weren't many places to pull over. The narrow road barely had room for two cars to pass if they were large. "There's a stand of saplings halfway down on left. If you veer toward them, we might stop before going over the cliff."

He cut her a quick glance. "We're heading for a cliff?"

"Unless you are positive we can make it down this mountain safely, then yes." She was out of her mind. He was too, if he agreed with her insane scheme.

"I'll decide when I see the grove." He turned the windshield wipers on high.

"Why would you drive up the mountain with defective brakes?"

"I didn't know they were defective."

"You're lying." She narrowed her eyes. "I can tell in your voice. You hesitated."

"Fine. The brake acted a little funny, but I didn't think they'd go completely out." He gave a one-shouldered shrug. "I promise to get you out of here in one piece."

"Ugh. You're unbelievable." Tears stung her eyes.

"You aren't going to faint, are you?"

"I told you my blood sugar was low yesterday from not eating." She glared at him. "Stop talking and watch the road." What if they fishtailed? A sharp curve loomed ahead of him. "Try hugging this side of the mountain. Maybe the gravel will grab the tires a bit."

"I know how to drive." He inched to her side, the tires crunching over rock.

The passenger-side mirror struck a low-hanging branch and was yanked off the vehicle. Another branch shattered her side of the front window in a myriad of spiderweb-type cracks. She bit her lip to keep from squeaking.

Sliding along the wall of the mountain did slow

them a bit, but not enough to pull them out of danger. Brynn's stomach roiled with another hairpin curve. The grove of saplings was still a couple of miles away—an eternity when the roads grew slicker with each minute the truck continued its mad dash down the mountain road.

Weston rolled his head, then squinted to see out the frozen window, his hands keeping a death grip on the wheel. Sweat beaded on his forehead despite the evening chill creeping through the widening cracks in the front windshield.

"Do you want me to turn the heater up?" Brynn reached for the knob.

"No. Turn it off, actually. This old truck isn't used to this abuse. The less we make it work, the better."

Another bump into the mountain and the windshield fell in pieces. Brynn turned off the heater. It wouldn't do any good without a way to keep the heat in anyway. She tugged her coat tighter around her, slunk down in her seat, and closed her eyes. She'd rather not witness the moment they flew off the mountain.

"You okay?"

"Positively divine." She kept her eyes closed tight.

"I'd take your hand, but I need both on the wheel."

"Absolutely." She took deep breaths through her nose and released them slowly out her mouth. Holding his hand sounded like a great way to feel secure. Another time. If there was one.

"How much further to the grove? The rain is making it hard to see."

She opened her eyes and studied the area. "One or two more turns, I think. You'll see a bit of grassy area, then the saplings. Please don't miss."

"I don't plan on missing."

They swerved around the next corner, the tail end of the truck coming dangerously close to the other side of the road where nothing would stop their perilous fall but trees and shrubs.

"There!" She tapped his arm and pointed.

"Hands off." He yanked the wheel to the left.

The rear of the truck slid, then righted as they barreled over the saplings. The truck slowed. A massive pine tree loomed in front of them.

Brynn screamed and put her arms over her head as the truck hit the tree. Her head whipped sideways, slamming against the passenger window. Everything went dark.

~

At least the pine tree stopped them from flying off the mountain. Weston glanced at Brynn to tell her so and try to relieve some of the tension from their out-of-control drive.

Her head leaned against the passenger door.

"Brynn?" He gave her a gentle shake. When she didn't respond, he tried exiting the truck. His door had crumpled too much for him to open it, so he climbed out the missing front window. "Brynlee?" He yanked on her door. It wouldn't budge. "Open your eyes, sweetheart." He patted her icy cheek. When she still didn't respond, he fished his cell phone from his pocket. No service. Could anything else go wrong?

Brynn groaned, and her eyes fluttered open. "What happened?"

"We crashed. Are you all right?" He moved her hair from her face. A purple knot rose on her temple.

"Killer headache." She stared out the window.

"Wow. Thank goodness for that tree."

He laughed. "That's a positive spin on things. Can you climb out the front window?" His smile faded. "Do you think you have a concussion?"

"I can try. As for the concussion, I have no idea." She put fingers to the knot on her head. With a sigh, she tossed out her purse and unhooked her seatbelt. "You should make sure your next vehicle has air bags."

"Of course." Although, he didn't plan on having any accidents in the future. Especially on purpose.

Brynn climbed out the window. He lifted her from the hood that resembled an accordion at this point.

"Do you have service on your phone?" He set her on her feet, catching her when she swayed.

"I never do up here." She leaned heavily against him.

From his best guess, he figured they were still at least five miles from the bottom of the mountain. "Can you make it down?"

"I don't really have a choice." She lifted a pale face to the cold rain and shivered. "Thank God for a wool coat. At least my torso is warm."

More than he could say for himself. "Come on." He put his arm around her waist. "You set the pace. We'll be fine."

"You really are a male version of Pollyanna, aren't you?" She frowned and let him help her to the road.

"Beats always looking on the bad side of things." Already his feet numbed against the icy blacktop of the road. His gaze fell to the thin shoes Brynn wore. She had to be as miserable as he was. He kept hoping for a car to come along, but hadn't seen one the whole time they'd been driving. Most people were smarter than him and Brynn. He should've checked the weather forecast. If he'd have known about the arriving icy conditions, he would've suggested a raincheck, faulty brakes or not.

The cold seeped to his bones making his teeth chatter. Brynn shivered so hard under his arm he thought she might break. They had to get out of the cold. The rain had stopped, turning his wet hair to icicles. He scanned the trees for a glimpse of light. Not seeing one, he tightened his hold on Brynn and increased their pace. "You holding up okay?"

"Ba...barely." She leaned into him. "We're going to die of hypothermia."

"No we aren't." He wouldn't let them. "Keep walking. We have to have gone at least a mile."

"Goo...goody. Only...three more to go."

Headlights cut through the trees, then blinded them as a car appeared from around the next corner. Weston had never been happier to see another person in his life. "We're going to be just fine, sweetheart."

The car stopped next to them. The driver's side window rolled down. "You folks need a ride? What happened?"

"Car accident." Weston opened the rear door. "We sure could use a ride into town. We're about frozen." He helped Bryn inside. "I'm Weston Hoover, and you're my new best friend."

"David Brown. Glad to meet you." The man wore a baseball cap pulled low over his face and the hood of a black sweatshirt pulled over that. The scent of an expensive cologne wafted from the car.

Weston didn't care what the man wore, smelled like, or whether he met his gaze. The important thing was that they were out of the weather.

~

He turned the heat higher, using more force than necessary. It hadn't occurred to him in the slightest that Brynlee would be in the chef's truck. It really hadn't occurred to him that they'd drive up the mountain in an ice storm. His plans could have gone very wrong.

"It's a good thing I showed up. It's going to start raining again any minute." He met the chef's glance in the rearview mirror. "You should be warm real quick."

"Thanks." He pulled Brynlee closer to him. "You live on the mountain?"

"Yep. Not a problem to turn around and take you where you need to go." He'd spotted the truck going up, but hadn't been able to follow until now. What he hadn't expected was to see the chef dead or bleeding in his truck, not walking with Brynlee. He'd have to be more careful with the next phase of his plan. "Where do y'all need to go?"

Brynlee recited the address he knew by heart. "I've an extra room, Weston, if you need to stay."

"Thank you, but I'll be needing dry clothes. I'll call for a ride. In the morning, I need to get my truck towed. Lucy isn't going to be happy to run the diner alone. I'd like to get everything taken care of in one day, if possible."

David's blood had started to boil as he envisioned the man staying at Brynlee's. His shoulders relaxed hearing he wouldn't spend the night. "I can drop her off, then take you. Not a problem. You'll catch your death if you don't dry off as soon as possible."

"We sure do appreciate you."

David glanced at the book on the front passenger

seat, then pulled a newspaper he'd bought over it. He didn't need Brynlee recognizing him. Once she figured out he copied the events between the book's pages, she'd tell the sheriff. "It's what small-town people do." He forced a grin. "We look out for each other."

Brynlee had fallen asleep, her beautiful head nestled on the man's shoulder. Weston shook her awake. "Can't go to sleep with that knot, sweetheart."

"She's injured? Maybe I should drive the two of you to the ER."

"I'm fine," Brynlee said. "I'm not seeing double or anything. And I don't feel nauseous—just tired."

David frowned, wishing he had the authority to convince her to seek medical treatment. "If you're sure." He pulled in front of her house.

"Let me walk her in," Weston said. "I'll be right back." He slid from the backseat and helped Brynlee out. A few minutes later, he climbed into the front seat, moving the newspaper and book into his lap. "I don't feel like an ice cube anymore. Thank you very much."

"My pleasure." Being nice was starting to wear on him. What he wanted to do was shove the chef into the street and run him over. Something he couldn't do because Brynlee would know it had to be him.

He contemplated driving past the man's house and into the fields outside of town. No, he needed to stick with the plan outlined in the book. His task had been to cut his brake line. He'd done that. Tomorrow's task was a new one.

When he stopped in front of the chef's house, the guy shoved open his door, replacing the paper and book back on the seat. "Next time you come to the diner, your meal is on me. Thanks again." He thrust out his hand.

David returned the shake, nodded, and drove away the second the man stepped back from the car. He hadn't made it very far in the book. Maybe there would be a way to get rid of Brynlee's male friend in the pages to come.

Chapter Five

David closed the book. He couldn't do it. No way could he run Brynlee off the road. He'd already done that the night before in a roundabout way.

Why was the antagonist in this book targeting the heroine and the man she was growing to love? Maybe he needed to read the whole book before setting plans in motion. Things needed to make sense after all. Oh, sure, he knew his reasons…he wanted to grab the attention of the woman he loved. But why did the character in this book do what he did?

Since the day was early and breakfast a couple of hours away, he opened the book again and started reading. By the time he'd finished, the sun perched above the horizon. Time to get moving. He needed another vehicle. Stealing from a nearby manufacturing plant wouldn't be difficult, and since he refused to harm Brynlee, he'd chosen her friend as a proxy.

The antagonist targeted the heroine because she'd rejected his declaration of love and moved quickly to the hero. Cliché, but obviously readers enjoyed the plotline. The bookstore owner had said the book came highly rated.

Thankfully, Brynlee hadn't done the same to him in spurning his love. By the time she knew who did these things for her, she'd want him as much as he wanted her.

~

Brynlee sat at her usual table at the diner and ordered an omelet. Even knowing Weston wasn't cooking this morning, she continued to cast quick glances into the kitchen.

"Considering the night Weston told me the two of you had, I'm surprised to see you out and about." Lucy set her order in front of her. "Thank goodness it's a slow day, or I'd never be able to keep up. One of the servers called in sick."

"I have to open up the library. This morning, I'm reading a Christmas book to the kids. Christmas is only a couple of days away. The library will be closed, and I'll catch up on my rest then." She smiled and picked up her fork. "Maybe Weston will make it in before the lunch rush."

"We can always hope." Lucy dashed back to the kitchen.

Surely it wouldn't take all day for Weston's truck to be towed down from the mountain. Brynn rushed through breakfast, grabbed her bag, and hurried to work. This morning, no one was waiting outside in the cold.

Inside, she stashed her bag in the bottom drawer of her desk and set up the children's nook with comfy pillows and beanbag chairs. A small Christmas tree glittered in the corner. A giant stuffed teddy bear wearing a Christmas vest invited a little one to snuggle.

The children started arriving at nine right along with a large bouquet of flowers. Tempted to read the card, Brynn set the arrangement on her desk and joined the children in the nook. The flowers would wait.

After story time, she thanked the children for coming, handed out oversized bookmarks, and wished everyone a Merry Christmas. A jingle from her desk drawer alerted her to a missed call.

She removed her cell phone from her purse. Several missed calls from Maddy and a text from Weston for her to call him. She dialed his number.

"Did you get your truck?"

"Yeah, but the news is disturbing."

"Oh?" She removed the card from the floral arrangement.

"The brake line was cut."

She drew in a sharp breath. "Are you sure?"

"Absolutely. 'A clean cut,' the mechanic said. I have no idea why anyone would do that to me unless it's in retaliation for following you through the park. Is this town that adverse to newcomers?"

"No, listen to this." Her gaze landed on the card, and she read, *"To my darling Brynlee. Someday, you will know the things I do for you. Someday we will meet face-to-face. Until that day, realize how much you are admired."* She frowned. "I received flowers from an anonymous admirer."

"Wow, I don't like the sound of that. I'm going to pay a visit to the sheriff's department. Want to go with me on your lunch hour?"

"Why? Do you think this is a threat?" Her throat threatened to close. Another ping came through. "Can you hold? I have another call."

"Sure."

She switched to the other line. "Sorry, Maddy, it's been a crazy morning."

"Thank goodness, I finally got through to you.

Brynn, someone ran me off the road. I'm stuck in a ditch over by Harper's farm. Can you come get me?" Maddy's voice seemed distant.

"Of course, but what do you mean someone ran you off the road? Are you hurt?" Her hand went to the knot on her head.

"Exactly that. A big, rusty truck sideswiped me." Her words caught on a sob. "It seemed like it was on purpose."

"I'll be there as soon as I can." She switched back to Weston, her voice trembling. "I need a ride now."

"On my way. I'm driving a rented navy-blue Corolla." He hung up without asking questions.

As much as she hated to, Brynn locked up the library. Friends came first. Always. And Maddy needed her.

Thoughts nagged at her as she waited for Weston. His brake line cut, Maddy's accident…the flowers now seemed sinister.

She unlocked the door and retrieved the card for the flowers before heading back outside. Since they'd be going to the sheriff's department, it wouldn't hurt to get Sheriff Westbrook's opinion.

Weston arrived five minutes later. His face grew serious as Brynn told him about Maddy. "This is all very strange."

"Like a book I just read." She told him about the happenings in the suspense novel. "But it's a little far-fetched to think someone is copying the plot, isn't it?"

"Time will tell. What should happen next?" He pulled from the curb and drove out of town.

Brynn searched her mind. "A dumpster fire. A homeless man died. We don't have many homeless people in Misty Hollow." She fiddled with the collar of her coat. Her suspicion couldn't be right. Why would someone torment her with a book she'd enjoyed? How would they have known about the book in the first place?

Unless that person was watching her. Brynn always read while eating at the diner. She cut Weston a frightened glance. "I think someone is watching me. The flowers are a threat. But why? The people of this town like me."

"Maybe it's someone new. They're also targeting me. Why? I thought at first it was because of the park incident, but now that they seem focused on you, too, I'm not so sure." He slowed the car. "There's your friend."

Maddy stood hunched against the cold next to her car. "Where's the tow truck?"

Brynn glanced at Weston. "We didn't call one. I never told Weston what the problem was until he picked me up."

"Get in the car where it's warm. We can call the tow truck from town. You don't need to wait out here." Weston opened the back door to the Corolla. "We're headed to the sheriff's office. I'm guessing you might want to join us."

"Definitely." Maddy gave a toss of her hair. "I can describe the truck in great detail."

~

Sheriff Westbrook listened without talking while the three of them took turns telling him why they paid him a visit. When they'd finished, he turned to Weston. "Roy is absolutely positive the line was cut?"

"Yes, sir. 'With a smooth blade,' he said." Weston

crossed his arms, anger rising fresh in his chest. "We could've been killed last night."

"The two of you were lucky. Brynn, let me see the card." He motioned for her to set it on his desk where he studied it without touching. "Definitely doesn't sound friendly or romantic to me. Maddy, I'm guessing the truck you're going to describe is an older model green Chevy with more rust than paint. Am I right?"

"Yes, but—"

"Reported stolen this morning. I'm certain the truck will show up with the paint from your car on the fender. I'll ask Doris to call a tow truck for you." He straightened in his seat. "Any idea why someone would try to kill the three of you?"

"Brynn seems to think this guy is following a book she read." Weston tilted his head. "Sounds far-fetched to me."

"But not unheard of. Brynn, anyone been showing you a lot of attention lately?"

She shook her head. "Just the guy from the Christmas party, but I haven't felt as if anyone has followed me anymore. I haven't met anyone new."

"What about the man who gave y'all a ride last night?" The sheriff arched a brow. "Ever seen him before?"

"Of course. At the diner and the library. He never made me feel uncomfortable, though. Am I missing something?" She paled.

Weston reached over and took her hand in his. "It's okay."

"Stop saying that. It's not okay." She narrowed her eyes at him before facing the sheriff again. "What do I need to do?"

"Stay alert. Don't go anywhere alone if you can help it. That goes for all three of you."

"Not me." Maddy leaped to her feet. "I'm headed to Little Rock to spend Christmas with my family. Try to catch this nut before I come back after New Year's, please." She darted from his office.

"That's an option," the sheriff said.

"I'm not leaving my home." Brynn's hand shook in Weston's. "Maybe this guy isn't as dangerous as he sounds."

"And maybe you didn't almost go for a flight off the mountain." Sheriff Westbrook folded his hands on the desk. "I'd like you to write down everything that happens in that book you mentioned. From the first to the last. Can you do that?"

"I can have it for you by the end of the day." She stood. "I need to go back to work."

Weston did, too. Lucy could use him, not to mention he needed to plan the Christmas Day menu for those who didn't want to cook at home or go to a friend's or family's house. He escorted Brynn back to the car and dropped her off at the library. "What are you doing on Christmas?"

"Eating at the diner. There's a handful of us who make it a yearly tradition." She slid out of the car. "You're cooking, right?"

He grinned. "You bet. It'll be the best Christmas dinner you've ever had. See you at lunchtime."

His smile faded when she entered the library. It had been bad enough believing someone wanted to harm him because they thought of him as a threat to Brynn, but knowing now that she was in as much danger as he was sent icy fingers down his spine.

It didn't make sense that someone would want to harm someone as sweet and kind as Brynn. Smart, beautiful—everyone he'd met in town liked her. It had to be someone new to town.

Before driving to the diner, he sent Brynn a text asking that she give him a copy of the book's plot points along with the sheriff. He wanted to stay alert.

Not only his life depended on it, but hers as well.

Chapter Six

Brynn tapped a silver bulb on her small tabletop Christmas tree on her way out the door. Merry Christmas, Misty Hollow. Her favorite holiday, even though she'd spent the last few alone other than dinner at the diner. She lifted her face to a light dusting of snow and smiled as the icy crystals kissed her cheek.

The weatherman had said there wouldn't be much snow, but even a tiny amount made the day that much more magical. She took a step forward, something crunching under her foot. She bent and picked up a white jeweler's box tied with a red velvet ribbon.

"What in the world?" She untied the ribbon and opened the box. A diamond tennis bracelet sparkled in the wintery mid-morning sun. Who would give her such a gift? Brynn glanced both ways. No one stood on the sidewalk in either direction. No cars passed on the silent street.

She peeked at the box again. A tiny card nestled under the lid that simply read, *From your admirer. See you soon.* Her blood chilled. Some of the day's specialness evaporated. Her stalker, the man who had tried to kill not only her and Weston, but Maddy, knew where she lived. He had been on her porch.

Her mouth suddenly dry, she stumbled against the door behind her. Had he come inside? Watched her sleep? She needed to go to the diner. She needed to be surrounded by friends. Brynn dropped the box and bracelet into her purse and took off at a run. Several people called out Merry Christmas as she entered Main Street, but she didn't stop. The sign of the diner had become a beacon of safety.

A horn blared as she darted across the street. She waved a hand in apology, then burst through the front door of the diner.

Lucy glanced up from the long table placed in the center of the room. A table runner with old-fashioned red trucks and Christmas trees stretched down the middle. White plates with red napkins steepled on placemats. "What's wrong?"

"Nothing. Is Weston in the kitchen?" Without waiting for her friend's answer, she shoved open the swinging door to the kitchen.

He spun around from basting the largest turkey Brynn had ever seen. "What happened?"

Tossing a glance over her shoulder to make sure they were alone, she stepped to his side and pulled the jeweler's box from her purse. "I found this on my porch. Read the card." Her hand trembled.

His gaze flickered from her to the card, and his eyes widened. "This was on your porch?"

"Yes." She swallowed against the lump in her throat. "I'm becoming scared. This is too close."

"I agree." A muscle ticked in his jaw as his gaze hardened. "I'm moving in with you until this is over. Merry Christmas. Looks like I'm your white-elephant gift."

Her mouth opened and closed several times as she tried to think of a way to say no, but he was right. She couldn't stay alone. Not until this crazy person was behind bars. Merry Christmas, indeed. "Okay. I'll make up the bed in the guest room after dinner." There were worse roommates out there.

When she turned to go, he put a hand on her arm. "We'll make it through this."

Sometimes, his always-optimistic attitude grated on her nerves. She scrunched her nose and joined Lucy to help finish the preparations for the holiday dinner.

By one o'clock, those either alone for the holiday or averse to cooking filtered through the door. Lucy, wearing a red dress and a frilly white apron, looked like a red-haired Mrs. Santa as she greeted her guests.

Brynn smoothed her deep green sweater over her black pants. Threads of gold twinkled from the fibers of the sweater. She pasted on a smile and greeted each of the newcomers. Was one of them her stalker?

Maybe Pete Lawrence? He'd asked her out several times, but the grease under his fingernails and lack of personal hygiene turned her off. What about David Brown? A newcomer to town. The man seemed nice enough. After all, he saved her and Weston from hypothermia, but nice on the outside didn't mean evil didn't lurk in his heart. Or Jim Orson. Another man who'd asked her out. She turned and smiled at his wife. Poor woman, stuck with such a pervert.

She kept the pleasant look on her face as they each scanned the place marks on the table and took their seats. Lucy had fancied up for the holidays.

Once everyone was seated, Brynn helped Lucy carry out the side dishes while Weston set the sliced turkey next to his plate at the head of the table. "Welcome, everyone, and Merry Christmas. Thank you for accepting me into this wonderful town. I look forward to becoming friends." Weston smiled from one face to the next, then said a short prayer before inviting everyone to start passing the dishes.

Laughter, jokes, and stories of past Christmases filled the air as everyone ate and celebrated. A few congratulations for a wonderful feast were tossed Weston's way.

The pleased expression on his face warmed Brynn's heart and took away some of the chill of the bracelet. Maybe he was right. Everything would be okay. She took a bite of sweet-potato casserole. Warm, gooey sweetness filled her mouth. Weston sure could cook.

The thought that he'd be cooking for her as her roommate came to mind only to be dismissed. He cooked for her every day since all her meals were at the diner. She'd never wanted to eat alone.

Brynn studied the faces around the table again. Sixteen in all. Friends of hers, she hoped. Her gaze stopped on the face of each man wondering if he could be the one who had sent her the bracelet. She received smiles and raised glasses as they met her gaze. The stalker couldn't be one of her friends.

Later that night, she faced the street decked out for the holiday, but this year it unnerved her. The snow continued to drift down with a laziness that made her want to curl up at home with a good book. Yet her stalker had to be out there, watching, waiting.

~

Why wasn't she wearing the bracelet? It took all David's willpower not to bring up the subject. Instead, he smiled, ate, and made small talk when all he wanted to do was spend the rest of Christmas Day alone with Brynn. Wasn't she pleased with the gift? It was a symbol of how much he cared about her. Instead, he had to share her with all the others and pretend to be having a good time. He cut a glance at Weston. The meal had been much better than David had expected. The man belonged in a five-star kitchen, not some hick diner in the middle of the Ozarks. Why was he here?

His ears perked at hearing Weston was a volunteer firefighter for Misty Hollow. A plan started to percolate in his mind as to how he could get rid of the man who appeared to be his competition. After he worked his way through the book, that is.

Who put out the stupid place markers? Given the chance, he'd have sat next to or across from Brynlee. Instead, she sat next to the chef three seats down—so far away he couldn't speak to her without yelling.

Which didn't stop the rest of the diners. They all shouted from one end of the table to the other as if none of them had good table manners. David shook his head and dabbed his napkin at his mouth.

"Everything okay?" Lucy arched a brow.

"Never better. I can't remember ever having a Christmas dinner this good."

"Thank you." Weston raised a glass of iced tea his direction. "That means a lot to me, especially after the way you helped Brynlee and me." He then went on to tell the others of David picking them up out of the freezing rain.

For several minutes, David basked in the adoration before putting up his hand. "I know everyone here would have done the same. That's what drew me to a town this size. The family atmosphere." True in some regard. He'd actually come to Misty Hollow to lessen the chance of discovery after the last woman he'd loved had not returned his affections. Unfortunately, he'd disposed of her after the rejection.

He hoped things would end differently with Brynlee.

~

The sun had begun its descent by the time Weston drove to his place to pack a bag, then took Brynlee home. His feet and back ached from hours preparing dinner and the cleanup afterward. Brynn looked as exhausted as he did. Still, it had been a wonderful day—the best he'd had in a very long time. "Did you enjoy yourself?" He asked as they headed to her front door.

"The food was wonderful." She scanned the area around her front porch, then mounted the steps and unlocked the door. "Good company, good food, good day."

Hopefully, it had been enough to shove aside thoughts of the gift she'd received. He wanted to ask her what she intended to do with the expensive bracelet but didn't want to arouse the fear he'd seen in her eyes that morning.

"Your room will be the last on the right." Brynn set her purse on the kitchen table. "I'll bring clean linens for you. There's only one bathroom on the left, but I think we can make it work."

"I'm perfectly capable of making the bed." He glanced around the surprisingly modern interior. A few antiques mixed with contemporary. Not a lot of knickknacks to clutter up the place. A multi-colored afghan covered the back of the sofa. It wasn't difficult to see Brynn living here.

She pulled a set of sheets from the closet and led the way down the hall where she set them on a bed with a colorful quilt covering it. Blinds covered the windows. A dresser and nightstand completed the décor. A few paintings of flowers covered the walls. "I hope you'll be comfortable. How about I make some coffee and meet you in the living room?"

"The room is perfect. I'll join you in a few minutes." He found the top dresser drawer empty and folded his clothes inside, setting his toiletries on top, hoping he wouldn't have to stay long. Staying for days—weeks—meant the danger to Brynn hadn't vanished. Tomorrow, he'd insist on taking the bracelet to the sheriff. When he'd finished, he headed for the living room where Brynn and cups of hot coffee awaited. She sat on the sofa, fuzzy socks on her feet, ankles crossed on the coffee table.

"I bet you're ready to sit." She motioned to the second cup.

"More than ready." He declined the vanilla-flavored cream, preferring his coffee black, and sat on the other end of the sofa.

"Volunteer fireman?" She tilted her head. "Are you really as nice as you seem to be?"

"What do you mean?" He took a deep breath of the aroma wafting from his cup.

"You are the most optimistic person I've ever met."

"Doesn't do any good to be pessimistic. Doesn't change anything." He took a deep breath. "I was engaged once. My fiancée died in a house fire. I couldn't save her. So—" he shrugged. "I became a volunteer fireman in hopes to keep the same from happening to someone else."

"I'm so sorry." She leaned over and put her hand on his arm. "I didn't mean to poke fun at your niceness. It's just I've never met anyone like you. Other than a shadow in your eye, you didn't retaliate when I accused you of being my stalker."

"Oh, I was pretty mad." He chuckled. "But, again, what purpose would showing my anger have accomplished?"

The doorbell rang.

"I'll get it." He set his cup down. "I know there's a peephole, but after this morning, I don't want you answering the door." He grabbed an umbrella from the stand and opened the door to see Sheriff Westbrook blowing on his hands. "Come on in before you freeze."

"Wicked cold tonight." He stomped the snow dust from his feet and entered.

"What is it?" Brynn stood at Weston's elbow.

"Afraid someone set fire to your truck, Weston. It's not salvageable. Burned part of the garage, too, before the fire was out. I decided to tell you in person as I'm on my way home to deal with a very unhappy wife that I'm working on Christmas."

His heart fell. He loved that truck. Weston cleared his throat. "Thanks for coming by. Are you sure it was set deliberately?"

"Yes. The arson left the gas can sitting right there. Made one heck of a bang. Surprised you didn't hear it. Sorry, man. And according to the list Brynlee gave me, it's going to be a burned building next time. Merry Christmas." He nodded and left.

Weston cast wide eyes on Brynn. If the arson was

her stalker, he could set the house on fire while they slept. It would be a repeat of Sybil, his deceased fiancé, all over again.

Chapter Seven

Weston didn't talk much on the way to the diner the next morning. It didn't take a genius to know the burning of his truck upset him. Or maybe it was the mention of fire. Her throat clogged remembering his sad story of how he lost his fiancée.

A yawn overtook her, shoving aside everything but the fact she needed another couple of hours sleep. For some insane reason, she'd insisted on going to the diner with him at the ungodly hour of five a.m.

"You really didn't have to come." He cut her a quick glance.

"Of course, I did. After the lecture from the sheriff last night about not going anywhere alone, it was either stay at home, which is not an option, or ride to work with you." The bitter cold from Christmas day hadn't left for one thing, and walking alone with a crazy person on the loose wasn't much better.

"The sheriff is right. Staying at home, working at the library, running errands—none of those are safe for you to do alone."

"The library is full of people all day." She stared out the passenger-side window. Danger or not, she would not become a prisoner in the diner, which she suspected would be Weston's idea of keeping her safe.

"How will you get to the diner for lunch?" He

tilted his head. "You'll have to walk or call for a ride."

"I'm not calling for a ride when it's across the street and half a block down." She frowned. "I'll be in sight of the diner the whole time. If the dude were to try and grab me, someone would see and shout an alarm. In a small town, no one is ever alone."

"Hopefully, you're right." He parked in front of the diner. "I don't want anything to happen to you."

"Same here. I'm not the only one this freak is fixated on."

He shrugged. "What are you going to do with the bracelet when the sheriff returns it?"

"Pawn or sell it." Brynn shoved her door open. A cold blast of air slapped her in the face. "I'll never wear the thing." She'd rather cut off her arm than wear the bracelet on her wrist.

"I don't blame you, but it looks expensive." He pressed the fob on the car, locking the doors.

Without a doubt, the bracelet cost a pretty penny. She laughed. "That's a sure sign you're from the big city."

"Habit." He grinned and put his hand on the small of her back, warming her through the wool of her coat.

Relieved he was talking again and that some of last night's sadness had left his face, Brynn kept a smile on her face as they entered the diner. "Good morning, Lucy."

"Good morning." She looked at them in surprise. "Am I missing something?" Her eyes narrowed. "Why are you here so early, Brynlee?"

She widened her eyes. How could she explain Weston had spent the night while also letting Lucy know their relationship was purely platonic?

"Brynn has a secret admirer who is getting a little too close," Weston said, taking the pressure off her. "I'm staying in her guest room until things settle down."

"Ah." Lucy nodded. "Here we go again."

Brynn's breath caught. For almost two years, she'd watched from the sidelines as trouble came to Misty Hollow. Now, it had come for her. Her legs gave way, and she plopped onto a chair. "Why me?"

Weston sat across from her and took her hands in his. "There's no way of knowing at this point. Somewhere you met someone who became infatuated with you. Either because of your niceness or your beauty. Maybe it's your killer smile." He cupped her cheek before taking her hands again. "That's not something you could've stopped."

"I'm a simple girl. There's no way I can deal with this." She lifted her gaze to meet his. "People die, Weston. Every. Single. Time."

"You're not going to be one of them." His grip tightened on her hands. "I won't let anything happen to you."

She wanted him to promise but knew it wasn't one he could keep. So, she nodded and got to her feet. "Since I'm here so early, you might as well put me to work."

"Brynn…"

"I'm fine." She forced a smile. "You're right. I couldn't stop the workings of a madman if I tried."

"Okay. I'm sure Lucy could use help rolling napkins around utensils."

"Awesome." She headed for the hostess station and set to work. The mindless task would help bury the worry that she was the next big story in Misty Hollow.

~

"What did you mean by 'here we go again'?" Weston pulled the pans he'd need for the breakfast rush from a shelf.

"Usually, a new gal arrives and brings trouble. This time, trouble came to one of ours. The town won't take kindly once they know." Lucy tied an apron around her flowered dress. "We had rival gangs back in the spring. Our very own motorcycle group helped bring them down. They'll rally again when they learn Brynn needs help. We've had the mob—that's part of the sheriff's story—stalkers, a deputy turned serial killer—you name it—and this poor town has dealt with it."

Thank goodness the motorcycle gang hadn't come after him when Brynn had made her accusation about him following her. "Vigilantes?"

"Not really. Just some good ole boys who like to help but occasionally get in the sheriff's way." She sighed. "What kind of trouble came to our Brynn?"

"Stalker. Seems he's following the plot of a book she read."

"For him to know what book she read, he'd have to have gone in her house." Her hand fluttered around her neck like a hummingbird.

"Yep." The thought made his stomach roll. "That's the reason I'm now staying with her."

"You're a good man, Weston." She clapped him on the shoulder. "I know you'll keep her safe."

Like he had with Sybil? "I sure hope so."

"Have faith, sweetie." She glanced to where Brynn filled a basket with the napkin-wrapped utensils. "We can't let anything happen to our girl."

Weston had a sneaking suspicion the motorcycle gang would be finding out about the threat soon. A suspicion confirmed when three leather-vested men arrived for breakfast and Lucy made a beeline for their table.

Several minutes later, the biggest of them entered the kitchen. "You staying with our Brynlee?"

Weston wiped his hands on a towel, then thrust one forward. "Yes, sir. Name is Weston Hoover."

"I know who you are." His gaze hardened. "She accused you once."

"A simple mistake." He squared his shoulders.

"You got a gun?"

"No."

"Heard you're a fireman. Reckon you know how to use an axe."

Weston frowned. "Reckon I do. What are you getting at?"

"You'll need a weapon when this man comes for her. Can you shoot?"

"Yes, I'm a pretty good shot."

"Good. Go to the pawn shop. Tell Harvey that Ben sent you. He'll make you a deal." He stared at the hand Weston still held out to him, then returned the shake, grinning. "Didn't mean to leave you hanging. I was focused on Brynlee is all."

"Can one of your men make sure she gets to work safely?"

"She'll always have a minimum of two tailing her. You can count on that." He gave a nod and returned to the dining room. "Larry, you and Rich make sure Brynlee makes it to the library. By then, our breakfast ought to be ready." His voice boomed across the diner.

"Real subtle, Ben." Brynlee's voice rose. "Let the whole town know, why don't you?"

Weston laughed and returned to cooking. She'd be okay now. Only a fool would take on a motorcycle gang.

"She'll be fine during the day," Lucy said, coming into the kitchen with three orders. "It's up to you to watch over her once she finishes working for the day. I'm thinking about hiring another chef so you can have some time off."

"I'm fine." He glanced at her in surprise.

"You work six days a week, Weston, and I pick up the slack when I need to. It's a lot for both of us." She grinned. "I'm sure most folks will come on the days you're working."

He shrugged. "Do you have anyone in mind?"

"I'm luring the chef from my rival over in Langsley." Her smile widened as she waltzed out the door.

He hadn't missed the sparkle in his boss's eyes. She had more than one reason to bring in a new chef, it seemed.

~

David cursed. He couldn't take on a bunch of leather-wearing thugs by himself. Appetite gone, he thrust his plate to the side, wishing he'd stayed at the hotel. But, Hoover was a better chef, and dining at Lucy's gave him the opportunity to feast his eyes on Brynlee.

He contemplated his next move as he sipped his coffee. Fire again. Abandoned building with a homeless man inside. Why homeless? He'd prefer it be someone who would be missed. But, he wouldn't deviate.

Setting the truck on fire, then watching the explosion, had given him a thrill like none other. He rather liked that the antagonist in the book used fire to catch the heroine's attention. Who knew the son of one of New York's elite would like playing with fire?

He tossed more money and tip than the server deserved, shrugged into his coat, and headed out into the snow—right behind Brynlee and two of the motorcycle goons.

When one of them glared over their shoulder, David jogged across the street. He'd circle the block before going to the library. He wanted to leave a message for Brynlee about how much he enjoyed the book they shared.

After spending a couple of hours in her presence, he'd scour the town for the perfect building, find his homeless man, then head back to the hotel and make final preparations for that evening. By asking some subtle questions, he'd found out that the homeless lived-in tents near the lake. It shouldn't be hard to find his victim. Anyone could be lured with the promise of money.

He ducked around the corner of the library and waited while his love's bodyguards stood until she stepped safely inside the building. After waiting a few more minutes for them to return to the diner, David entered the library.

"Good morning." Brynlee slipped out of her coat and draped it over the back of her chair. "Looking for anything in particular today?"

"Thought I'd browse the new-release section for a good thriller." He smiled and headed that way.

"I can recommend something if you'd like." She followed him, making his heart soar.

He caught a whiff of a musky perfume and closed his eyes for a second to soak it in. "That would be great. Thanks."

She pointed a couple out to him. "You might not want to turn the lights out after reading these." Her laugh sounded like music to his ears.

"I'm not afraid of the dark per se." He smiled. "It's the things *in* the dark that can hurt you."

Something like fear flickered in her eyes.

"Just kidding. I don't confuse fiction and real life." How easy the lie fell from his lips. "Thanks." Not wanting to risk her becoming skittish, he headed for the checkout desk. He couldn't take any chances of her knowing who her admirer was until he was ready.

Chapter Eight

Weston's phone blared at the same time Brynn's let out a jingle.

She gasped, paling.

He glanced at his screen. A call to fight a fire. His heart dropped.

"What's your text about, Brynn?" He sent Lucy a text that she'd have to cover the breakfast crowd, then pocketed his phone. Maybe she was right about needing another chef. "You look as if you've seen a ghost."

"I received a 'you're welcome' message from an unknown number." She raised wide eyes to him. "The next thing that happened in the book was a warehouse burned down with a homeless man inside."

He didn't think his heart could drop any further when he dove to his feet. "I've got to go, Brynn. Call Sheriff Westbrook and let him know." He cupped her face. "I don't want to leave you."

"You're needed somewhere else. I'll be fine. Look outside." She reached behind her and parted the curtains.

Three men on Harleys waited at the curb. Weston chuckled. "You couldn't be any safer."

"They promised me a ride." Her eyes twinkled as she planted her hands flat on his chest. "Now go."

He gave a nod and grabbed his coat, torn between

obligation and desire. Knowing he couldn't be with Brynn twenty-four-seven rankled. Outside, he let the bikers know where he was headed and received promises they'd see Brynn safely to the diner, then to the library. Weston couldn't do anything more than that.

He sped toward the address given, wishing he'd taken time to buy another truck. A four-door sedan wasn't his dream car, and this one wasn't nearly fast enough in an emergency. Not with its little four-cylinder engine.

By the time he arrived at the warehouse, the fire blazed around the metal roof. Firemen held hoses to the flames. The sheriff stood off to the side with the fire chief.

Weston rushed their way to suit up and determine what they wanted him to do. "Did Brynn let you know there is most likely someone inside?"

The sheriff's features grew sterner. "Yep. The fire's too hot to go in. The building will be a total loss."

Weston started putting on his gear. "I'll head around to the back." If there was a way in, he'd take it.

"Don't do anything stupid." The sheriff narrowed his eyes.

"What makes you think I would?"

"I don't know you well enough to know much, but you seem the type to want to play hero."

He definitely wasn't a hero. Weston grabbed an axe and took off at a run toward the back of the building where two firemen streamed water onto the roof.

"It's going to come down soon," one of them said.

"There's someone inside." Weston slammed the

axe into the back door. The impact of metal on metal vibrated up his arms.

"You'll never make it out," the other man said.

"I have to try."

After several whacks on the handle, he kicked the door open. "Hello? Anybody in here?" He stepped into an inferno, praying he wasn't making a mistake.

The warehouse looked like one cavernous space with a few doors along its walls. It would be suicide to enter any of those rooms. He'd have to stick to the main part of the building.

He glanced overhead. Steel beams held up a metal roof. Fire ate at the steel, climbing up the walls, but not really burning through the concrete. More like the burning off of alcohol when making flambé.

The arsonist had to know it wouldn't be easy to bring down a building with little wood in its structure. Weston peered through the thick smoke. The fire chief ordered him out of the building.

"I'm perfectly safe, sir. The fire is staying to the accelerant used." Weston spotted a man slumped against the wall. "I found the person inside. I'm bringing him out."

Removing a glove, he felt for a pulse. Finding one, he slung the man over his shoulder and headed for the door. "He's alive." His mind spun. The man the sheriff sought was playing some kind of sick game, but why set a fire that wouldn't do the job intended? Brynn needed to let him see that book.

Outside, he transferred the homeless man into the capable hands of the waiting paramedics and removed his gear. While he did, he explained what he'd seen inside. "Brynn received a text this morning that simply said, 'you're welcome.' Could be the perp's way of letting her know he purposely didn't kill this man." He gestured to the gurney.

"Then why set the fire at all?" The fire chief shook his head. "Some people make no sense at all."

"It's from a book." Sheriff's Westbrook's answer came out as a growl. "Except I'm guessing the victim died in the book. We must catch this guy before someone does die." He stormed to his waiting vehicle.

"Looks like you're a hero after all." The fire chief jerked his thumb toward a news van. "Here comes the blond vulture."

~

Brynn watched with her mouth hanging open as a fireman carried a lifeless body from a burning building. Her skin prickled when the fireman removed his helmet to reveal Weston's face.

"I knew he's a good man." Lucy watched the live news report with her and the other morning diners.

The reporter, Jane Moreland, thrust a microphone in Weston's face. "What made you run into a burning building, Mr. Hoover?"

"It's my job." His brow furrowed.

"The others weren't going in."

"I knew someone was inside."

"How did you know?" She stepped closer to him. "An anonymous tip?"

Weston now looked like a deer caught in headlights. "No comment." He practically ran to his car.

"He's so cute." Lucy chuckled. "Almost spilled the whole beans about this kook, didn't he?"

"But, he didn't." Brynn hitched her purse on her

shoulder and joined the men waiting on their motorcycles. She'd declined the offer of a ride because of the cold wind, but planned on taking them up on their promise on the first warm day.

So, she walked with the bikes rumbling along beside her on the way to the library. With promises to return at noon, they roared away the second she stepped into the building.

Her phone rang. A quick glance of the screen showed Maddy called.

"I saw the news."

Brynn laughed. "Hello to you too."

"You're going to grab that hunk with both hands, right? Because if you don't, I will."

"Stop it. We're just friends. He's staying with me until—"

Maddy's squeal cut her off. "He's staying with you? Spill the beans. I'm bored to tears at my parents' house."

"There's nothing to tell. Think of him as my bodyguard." She plopped into her desk chair. Gotta go. Hopefully, you can come back soon."

"Okay, but if you kiss that hero man, then you'd better do some telling. Bye." Maddy hung up, leaving Brynn with a smile on her face.

If she were honest, she'd admit to enjoying Weston as a houseguest. Having company each night when she returned home after supper, not going back to an empty house—yeah, she'd liked him there. The smell of his cologne after he showered. The rumble of his laughter when she said something funny.

It wasn't until he started staying with her that she realized how lonely she'd been since her parents started traveling the world. Not that she lived with them. She'd bought this house five years ago, but she had spent a lot of time with them. Then she'd started eating her meals at the diner. At a small table, alone, with a book for company. How things had changed with Weston's arrival.

A young man carrying a bouquet of yellow roses entered the library. "You Brynlee?"

She swallowed against a throat that had gone dry and nodded.

"Here you go." He flashed a grin, handed her the flowers, and left the library whistling.

Her hand trembled as she reached for the card and read, *I didn't kill the man for you.* What now, God? She grabbed the phone on her desk and called the sheriff. Within the half hour, deputy Hudson, a rookie who didn't look old enough to shave much less work in law enforcement, arrived.

"Sorry, Sheriff is working on the arson case." He held out a paper sack. "Drop the card in here. We'll send it to the lab, although I doubt the person who sent these even touched it."

Brynn was more than happy to get rid of the thing. "Throw these flowers out, too, okay? Please?"

"Sure thing." He scooped up the arrangement and left.

"Those sure were pretty flowers." David Brown leaned against her desk.

"Secret admirer." She shuddered.

"Scared?"

She tilted her head. "Maybe. Why all the questions? Wouldn't you be worried if someone sent you flowers, and you didn't know who?"

"No, ma'am, I'd be honored that someone felt that way about me."

She took a deep breath through her nose. "Did you finish the three books from yesterday?"

"No." He smiled. "The internet is out at the hotel, so I have some work to do."

"What kind of work do you do?" A good librarian knew about her regulars.

"Business."

His evasive expression didn't invite more questions. "Well, let me know if I can help you with anything." Keeping her smile in place, she turned to her computer to start checking in returned books.

~

He had a whole lot of things she could help him with. Unfortunately, it wasn't time to let her know about them. Soon, though. Very soon.

He tamped down the anger at seeing the deputy walk out with the flowers he'd sent Brynlee. Sending the card to the authorities was a given. They wouldn't find any prints. The order had been called in by the concierge at the hotel. David hadn't used his real name or the David Brown one. Making up names came so easy, and most people didn't question things. Especially at a fancy hotel that seemed out of place in Misty Hollow.

Who'd built the place anyway? The same people who had wanted a resort and casino? Some mob boss. He'd done his research before arriving at the hotel for a convention in Langley. The conference hotel had been booked up, so he'd been forced to find a room in Misty Hollow. Exactly as it was meant to be. Coming to this town had led him to Brynlee.

Since he had enough money to live well for several years, he had all the time needed to make her fall in love with him.

Which she would. He had no doubt. Because the last step in the book was for them to be together.

He bit back a laugh at what he'd witnessed on the news. Yes, he'd deviated a bit from the plot by not burning down the building with the man inside, but this story needed a hero, so he'd created one. A hero that he would rid the world of before taking the girl.

Chapter Nine

Since the new chef, a man named Greg Payson, had started work at the diner, Weston had a rare day off. "Want to go with me to pick out a truck? We could grab lunch in Langley."

Brynn glanced up from the book she read. "Why don't you go to the garage?"

"He doesn't have anything to sell right now. Besides, I'm overdue for a brand-new ride." He grinned. "I've never had a vehicle that wasn't pre-owned."

She closed the book. "Sure. I could grab some things from the grocery store. Give me ten minutes."

Taking her mind off her stalker, even for a day, was the primary reason for inviting her along. Second was the fact he enjoyed her company and looked forward to spending a day with her. They could both use some time away from the danger Misty Hollow held for her.

She'd changed out of yoga pants into jeans and a sweater the same shade of light blue as her eyes. Her dark hair bounced around her shoulders as she headed for the front door, leaving a trail of floral perfume in her wake.

Grabbing her coat, Weston helped her put it on before donning his own. "Let's have a day of shopping therapy."

She laughed. "I've never heard a man say those words before."

"You must not have been with a man shopping for a truck." Or a gun. Something else he intended to purchase. "We can even go to the mall if you want." He opened the front door and froze.

Red ribbon and evergreen boughs decorated the porch railing. Twinkling lights hung from the roof. Unless Brynn had gotten up after he went to bed, these were not here the night before.

"Okay? Now he's decorating my house?" She glanced up at him. "That doesn't seem too threatening. It's definitely not part of the book, though."

"It's threatening in the fact that he did all this without us knowing." He wanted to yank it all down, even reaching for the nearest bough, but stopped. If Brynn kept spurning his gifts, the man might retaliate with violence toward her. So far, he didn't seem to want her harmed. More like he was courting her. "Let's leave it. Maybe you should adopt a dog."

"But, it's after Christmas." She frowned. "The neighbors will say something, and I'm allergic to dogs, unfortunately. I'd love to have one."

"A lot of people leave their decorations up until January 6th. It'll be fine." He put his hand on the small of her back and guided her to the rental car.

Inside, she faced him. "What is he trying to do?"

"Get you to notice him, maybe. It has to be someone you know."

"That's scarier than the guy being a stranger, but I've thought the same thing. I study everyone who comes in the diner or the library." She sighed. "But no one looks the slightest bit suspicious."

"We'll find out who he is." Weston would make sure of it. One way or the other, they'd find the culprit and stop him before he harmed Brynn.

The thirty-minute drive to Langley was mostly silent as the two stayed in their thoughts. With the worry niggling at Weston's mind regarding Brynn's stalker, he could only imagine what she thought about it all.

"If I knew who it was," she said as they strolled across the car lot in Langley, "then I could ask him what he wants from me. If he wants a date, then I'd be happy to oblige. Then, we'd have time to discuss his reasons for scaring me."

"Sweetheart." He turned her to face him. "Not even a crazy kook goes on this long, stalking someone for a mere date. He wants something more." Possibly her life.

She paled. "Wouldn't he have harmed me already?"

"Did the bad guy in the book?"

Her eyes widened. "Not until the end. Then, he kidnapped her and…"

"And what?" His heart skipped a beat.

"Nothing. He was in love with her and wanted her to feel the same."

She was leaving something out, but he didn't press. He'd found the book on her bookshelf last night and had every intention of starting it that evening. Then, they'd stay one step ahead of the creep.

Why wasn't a deputy making regular drive-bys? If they were, they'd have seen whoever hung the decorations. Weren't small towns full of nosy people?

"We should ask your neighbors whether they saw anyone."

"Great idea." She stepped aside so he could push open the door to the dealership. While Weston picked out his new ride and quibbled with the salesman over the price, she meandered among the other cars for sale.

If she didn't live so close to everything she needed, she could use a new car. As it was, her car had little mileage and was still in perfect shape.

Movement outside the large wall of windows caught her eye. She glanced up, almost positive a man ducked out of sight when she looked. When she looked again, they were gone, as if no one had been there in the first place.

Stop being so paranoid, Brynlee. She couldn't expect the stalker to be everywhere she went. Surely, the man had a job. She glanced again. Not seeing anyone but a salesman talking to a man on the opposite side of the lot, she turned as Weston signed papers in front of him. He'd purchased a wine-colored Ram truck.

Finally. Her stomach growled.

Weston stood, a set of keys dangling from his index finger. "Would you mind driving the rental to the lot? I'll lead the way, then we'll grab lunch."

"I don't mind at all." She caught the keys he tossed her way. "You look as happy as a child at Christmas."

"I am. This baby comes with a heavy price tag, but she should serve me well for a long time."

Brynn glanced in the rearview mirror several times, spotting a dark car that seemed to be following them. Of course, Langley being the size it was, and busy despite being the middle of the day, the guy in the vehicle could simply be a driver headed toward the mall.

With everything that had happened lately, she chose not to believe she was being followed.

~

The salesman hadn't been happy when David didn't buy a car. He'd had to pretend to be interested for a while after Brynlee almost caught him watching her through the window.

It shouldn't surprise him that she'd be alert to her surroundings. She wasn't stupid by any means.

He drummed his fingers on the steering wheel as he followed Brynlee. He wanted to tell her his real name was Peter Drury. But she'd grow suspicious if he told her he was in town using an alias. Well, soon, she'd know the real him.

When Weston and Brynlee pulled into the rental-car lot, he drove on past and pulled in the shade of a larger building to wait. When they left, he'd slip in behind them and continue following.

The antagonist in the book had started shooting in a public place. Peter could have gone into the rental agency, but the place was too small for any anonymity. No, it had to be somewhere larger, full of people, where he could shoot and run.

His gaze landed on the automatic rifle on the passenger side of his car. He wasn't a fan of guns, but he'd said he would finish the plot of the book, and he would.

It had pleased him to see she hadn't taken down the decorations. He'd spent a good two hours hanging them—something he'd thought of on his own. The book didn't dictate everything he did.

He straightened in his seat as Weston, Brynlee, and woman in black slacks and a yellow tee-shirt with the rental emblem exited the building and circled the car. A few minutes later, Weston signed the clipboard and escorted Brynlee to his new truck.

Peter laughed. He'd make sure the pretty truck didn't look so pretty for long.

His smile widened when the truck pulled into the parking lot of the mall. He'd found his shooting place.

~

"I hope you like food-court food." Weston opened the door to the mall where they were immediately assaulted by many conversations at once.

"I'm not picky." She smiled up at him. "It won't be your cooking, though."

"Nothing is, sweetheart." He guided her to where several vendors circled the food court. "Anything strike your fancy?"

"Kung Pao chicken."

"Oh, you like it spicy." He arched a brow.

"I do."

"I'm a bit of a wimp, but I like the orange chicken." He let her precede him in line. "Are you looking for anything in particular at the mall?"

"Clearance racks." She laughed. "I like nice clothes, but I don't like the price tag. So, clearance racks are my friend whenever I make it to the mall."

Weston wanted to buy her anything she wanted. He'd made really good money as chef in a four-star restaurant. In fact, he made enough to live comfortably while working at Lucy's. What good was his money without someone to share it with? After Sybil's death, he'd quit his fancy job. Yes, he still loved being a chef, but the glitz and glamour of fancy food had lost its appeal. Brynn might be the one to bring all that back to him.

When they had their food, they headed for an empty table. He'd barely had time to sit before shots rang out, followed by screams. He shoved the table out of the way and tackled Brynn to the ground. "Is this part of the book?"

"Not exactly." Her eyes widened. "The shooting took place at a grocery store."

"Well, you're not at a grocery store." He lifted his head to take note of the exits. The one they'd entered through. The one that was now blocked by a man in a dark hoodie and ski mask. The other door had to be further down the mall.

He yanked Brynlee to her feet. "Stay close. Don't let go of my hand. We have to make sure we're surrounded by people."

She nodded, her face pale. Her hand trembled in his, but the resolve in her eyes let him know she wouldn't freeze up.

Those in the food court merged into one large, frantic group, breaking up when they cleared the food vendors. Half went one way, half the other. Weston turned right with the largest group.

"No." Brynn tugged on his hand. "The door is closer this way."

"Lead the way." Keeping as low as possible, they joined the group fleeing to the left.

A middle-aged man fell, a red stain spreading across his chest. Then a woman, covering her child with her body. More people fell.

A bullet tugged at Weston's shirt. He pulled Brynn

into a bookstore. "Stay down."

She nodded, taking refuge behind a display of children's books. "In the story, the shooter is trying to get to the hero. That would be you. He's reached the point of the book where he wants the love interest out of the picture."

"I like being the love interest." He winked. "Do I make it out?"

"Yes. The cops show up, but the shooter escapes." She gripped his shirt. "He'll try again."

"Nothing will happen to me as long as you help me stay one step ahead."

More shots fired, then shouting. Best he could tell, the cavalry had arrived. Weston straightened to peer over the display. The shooter, minus his weapon, sprinted past their hiding place. He shoved aside anyone foolish enough to get in his way. More shots fired, from the police this time. Hopefully, they'd get lucky and, unlike the book, the shooter wouldn't escape.

Five cops gave chase. "Come on. Let's get out of here while your stalker is busy." He grabbed her hand and raced for the door through which they'd entered the mall.

At his truck, they jumped inside and sped away. No more going anywhere until this guy was caught. "Nowhere but the diner, work, and home from now, Brynn." He cut her a stern glance. "I don't want to be overbearing, but it's too dangerous."

She nodded, tears filling her eyes. "Today could have ended very differently. He's following the book, but that doesn't mean he wouldn't have killed you if he had the opportunity."

Weston would make sure the man never had the chance.

Chapter Ten

Sheriff Westbrook stood on Brynn's porch and stared at the decorations. "I think you should take them down."

"Won't that anger this guy?" Weston crossed his arms.

"Maybe. It might also draw him out. The more he comes around, the better our chances of catching him." He exhaled heavily. "Seems he's following the book, but not exactly. The next thing on that list is that Brynlee will receive flowers and a love letter. I'll post a deputy outside your house and the library, although I doubt we'll catch him. He's smart enough to have them delivered."

Brynn wrapped her arms around her middle to get rid of the chill that had swept through her body. She wanted this all to be over, but she knew the ending. The shining star in knowing meant she could prevent the hero from being injured almost to the point of death. That meant, he'd be coming after Weston before taking her. Hopefully, she could help the sheriff stay one step ahead of this psycho.

She reached up and grabbed the nearest strand of greenery, yanking it down with more force than necessary. Brynn hoped the man was watching. She hoped his blood boiled. Tossing the strand into the yard, she glanced up and down the street. *Are you watching, you sicko?*

With a concerned glance her way, Weston helped remove the decorations as the sheriff strode back to his vehicle. "You okay?"

"Just peachy." She tossed aside a red velvet ribbon. When they'd finished and tossed everything into the large black trashcan next to the house, Weston drove them to the diner.

"Brynlee, this is Chef Greg Payson. Chef, this is Brynlee Bourge, the town librarian," Weston introduced.

"She doesn't look like a demure librarian." The burly man thrust out his hand. "I see a spark in them blue eyes."

"Falling into the trap of a cliché is dangerous." Brynn laughed and returned his shake. "Glad to meet you."

"Well, I'm off until the supper crowd." His gaze warmed as it landed on Lucy. "See you then."

Brynn smiled. Ah, Lucy had an admirer. Still smiling, she headed for her usual table near the kitchen and requested biscuits and chocolate gravy.

"Why aren't you fat?" Lucy shook her head. "As often as you eat the chocolate, you ought to be as big as that bull of Henderson's."

"Good metabolism." She pulled a book from her bag and started to read. "Oh, with lots of butter, please."

"You got it, darlin'." Weston tossed her a wink and entered the kitchen.

His endearments never failed to send her heart fluttering. Brynn set down her book and stared into space. She'd grown accustomed to being alone. Rarely dated. Not that she hadn't been asked, but because she'd never been tempted. Her gaze flicked to the swinging kitchen door. Weston tempted her. A lot.

She licked her lips imagining him kissing her. Their friendship remained platonic. What if he didn't feel anything more for her? Maybe he only spent time with her out of a sense of chivalry.

Her heart sank. What was it about her that put most men off? She was pretty enough. Nice. A bit shy. Her mouth fell open. Did people take her shyness for aloofness? The residents of Misty Hollow seemed to like her. Most treated her like a little sister. That was it. The men of this town didn't want to date their little sister.

"Hmph." Neither did newcomers, it seemed. She returned to her book. The one thing that would never forsake her was a good story. If the only romance available to her was within the pages of a book, then so be it. The thought saddened her, and her eyes traveled to the kitchen door again.

"Brynlee?" The hostess's voice drifted across the room. "She's at that table over there."

Her heart stopped as a young man carried a large bouquet of red roses toward her. He smiled and set the flowers on the table. "Someone must really like you."

With shaking fingers, she plucked the envelope from inside the bouquet and opened it with the knife wrapped in a napkin. She had to read what the letter said, knowing it would be verbatim what she'd read in the book, but she wanted to leave as few fingerprints as possible.

"Read that in the kitchen." Lucy gripped her arm.

"People are staring. Don't give them anything more to gossip about."

"You're right." Brynn grabbed the flowers and carried them and the letter into the kitchen.

Weston's face hardened at the sight of the roses. He wiped his hands on a towel and waited for her to read.

"I'll call the sheriff," Lucy said.

Brynn nodded and started to read. "*My lovely darling. Every time I lay eyes on you, it's as magical as the first time I spotted you across the room and knew instantly that you belonged to me.*" She swallowed against the growing boulder in her throat.

Weston handed her a glass of water. "You don't have to read it out loud."

"I want you to know what it says." She took a sip and continued. "*Every day, I soak in your beauty, your kindness, the love of the people around you. It won't be long now before I introduce myself, and we can start living as one. Or dying. Your choice. Your never-ending admirer.*"

~

"So, he'll do a murder suicide if you rebuke him?" An icy fist clenched Weston's heart, stealing his breath.

"Yes. These are the very words he used in the book." She slipped the letter back into the envelope.

"I read the ending of the book last night." He'd skipped to the last couple of chapters. "I'm guessing the gal went along with him until the very end."

"She had to in order to save the life of the man she loved."

Who did Brynn love? It couldn't be him. He'd never allow himself to love a woman again. His fondness for Brynn grew every day, but love? No. He wouldn't allow it. What an idiot. His heart knew different. She'd come to mean more to him than he'd thought possible.

"Sheriff's here." Lucy held the swinging door open.

"That was fast," Weston said.

"I happened to be on my way to grab some breakfast." He stared at the flowers. "Letter?"

Brynn handed it to him by the corner. "Same words as in the book."

"How many more steps do we have?" Weston glanced from her to the sheriff. "Can I have a copy of that list?"

The sheriff pulled out his cell phone. "Just texted it to you." His somber eyes landed on Weston. "The danger to you is going to increase. The perp wants you out of the picture, and he'll keep going until he has you."

Weston hitched his chin. "What happens if we go through all the steps, and I'm still here?"

The sheriff gave a wry smile. "Let's hope you're around so we can find out. I'll take the flowers and the note to the station, although we all know there won't be any prints other than the florist's and delivery guy's."

Jane Moreland burst into the kitchen followed by her cameraman. "Why does the sheriff have flowers intended for Brynlee? What's going on here?" She thrust a microphone in Brynn's face.

"No comment," Brynn muttered.

"The citizens have a right to know if there's danger."

"She said 'no comment.'" Weston put his arm

around Brynn's shoulder. "Please leave. We've diners to feed."

"Why are there two motorcycle guys waiting to escort Brynlee to the library?" She tilted her head. "What kind of danger are you in?"

"That's enough." Lucy kept moving forward forcing Jane out of the kitchen. "No one but chefs in the kitchen."

"Brynlee's not a chef." Jane glared.

"She's my girl." Weston tightened his hold. "That gives her the right." He ignored the shocked look Brynn tossed his way.

"I'll get the story one way or the other." Jane stomped away, her heels clattering on the tiled floor. At the door, she turned. "I always get the story."

The diner had fallen silent and now erupted into many conversations at once as everyone peppered Lucy with questions. Weston shook his head. "Stay here. I'll send your escorts to the back door."

She nodded and sagged against the counter. "Thank you."

Weston left the kitchen and headed for the two men standing like massive bookends near the door. "She'll be going out the back today, boys," he said softly.

"Gotcha." They returned to their bikes which roared to life.

Weston grabbed Brynn's book and bag on his way to the kitchen. "Let me package your breakfast order. You're already late opening the library. A few more minutes won't matter."

"Everyone will be coming in to ask questions. What do I tell them?"

"The truth. You have an admirer that's coming a little too close. It doesn't hurt to have extra eyes looking over you." He put the biscuits and gravy into a to-go box and handed it to her. "I'll see you at lunch."

"Be careful," she whispered. "You're the primary target now." She turned and left out the back door.

Weston watched as she climbed onto the back of one of the motorcycles, her bag over her shoulder, and her breakfast clutched in her hands. The driver saluted him and pulled away from the building. With a quick glance up and down the pavement behind the diner and not seeing anything suspicious, Weston closed the door and locked it behind him. Orders had piled up by the time he returned to the stove, and he got to work with a vengeance.

"Do you want me to call Greg in? He won't mind helping you catch up." Lucy pulled a pan of biscuits from the oven. "Luckily, we have both servers working today, and that frees me up to lend a hand."

"I think we have it." He cracked eggs for an omelet. "Folks won't mind sticking around a bit to gossip about what could be happening with Brynn."

Everything in him wanted to lock her somewhere safe. Just the two of them until this blew over. Unfortunately, that couldn't happen. This man wouldn't simply go away. He had a mission, and that meant getting rid of Weston and claiming Brynn.

He whisked the eggs a bit rougher than necessary, then poured them into a pan adding peppers, onions, ham, and cheese. They needed a plan to lure the man out of hiding, coerce him to stop following the book, and step into the open where the authorities could nab him.

The toaster released its bread, causing him to jerk.

"Sorry." Lucy grinned and slathered the pieces with butter.

Weston took a peek at the sheriff's text. Someone who'd bothered the main character would be killed. Who could that possibly be? Everyone loved Brynn.

~

Peter watched the drama in the diner. It pained him to see Brynn spurn his gifts, but they were all part of the plan. She'd read the same book he had. Brynn knew how the story ended. Only she could change the ending. All she had to do was accept him.

If not, he was fully prepared to die along with her. That's what a man did who loved as deeply as he. When the woman you loved was gone, there was no more point in living.

No worries. He dumped cream in his coffee. Once she knew who he was, saw the lifestyle he could give her, she'd be more than happy to leave this Podunk town for a luxurious life.

His spoon dinged the sides of his cup as he stirred. A server brought him his ham and cheese omelet.

"Sorry it's late, sir. The chef is catching up now."

"That's all right. Things happen. It won't affect your tip." He smiled and dug into his breakfast. After he ate, he'd move to the next step. Who knew he'd enjoy the act of killing as much as he did? The thrill was like a drug. Would he be able to stop once Brynlee was his?

Chapter Eleven

It didn't take long for Peter to find his target. The downtown area of Misty Hollow wasn't that big. After all, a reporter would either be out harassing people for a story or in the office. He found her sitting in her car at the newspaper office talking on her cell phone.

He peered around to see whether there were any cameras. None that he could see. Not that it mattered. He'd changed into his ski mask and hoodie.

The knife in his hand screeched along the side of the car as he made his way to her window. Though he wanted to linger and savor the kill, that would put him at risk of being seen. He yanked open the door and slit her throat before her eyes could register what was happening.

The phone fell from her fingers as she clutched her throat. Blood gurgled from the slash.

Peter hung up the phone, then darted away.

The reporter was the only person he'd been able to think of that could have been even the slightest nuisance to his love. She wouldn't be missed much. Reporters were like vultures, stretching the truth for drama. Well, she had her story now.

Grinning he drove his car to the next thing. A little

warning for the chef. He laughed, having the best time of his life. How different things would have been if he hadn't spotted Brynlee at the Christmas party. He'd be back in New York working and bored out of his mind. Now, he had a purpose. A reason to wake up every day other than making more money.

~

A steady stream of people came into the library that morning. Brynn told each of them the same thing. She had an admirer that took things a step too far. Multiple people promised to watch out for her.

Their concern warmed her heart, but the constant questions wore her down. She should've closed the library that day. Called in sick. She'd tried for over a year to convince the town to hire another librarian, but there wasn't any room in the budget. If she didn't show up for work, the library didn't open.

June Mayfield, one of the town's older residents, bustled into the library. "If you aren't in here to use the computers or rent a book, get out. This poor girl isn't a sideshow."

"What are you doing out of your house?" Brynn smiled as people drifted from the building. "You rarely venture out."

"I had to pick up a prescription and saw all the cars in the lot." She leaned on the counter. "You know as well as I do that most of those people rarely pick up a book."

Brynn laughed. "Thank you for rescuing me."

"As you know, this town has had its share of stalkers. Just remember this—" She tapped her finger on the counter. "Good will prevail as always."

"People died, June."

"People die every day. Don't be one of them." She moved around the counter and sat in the vacant chair where a second librarian would sit if the town had one. "Now, you need to think and think hard. You probably know this fool. Anyone asked you out lately?"

"No."

"Town's full of idiots. Okay, any newcomers?"

"Weston." Brynn bit the inside of her lip. "David Brown, but he's too nice to be a stalker. The man loves to read, too." Brynn gasped. "My stalker read the same book I did and is following it to a T. Do you think it could be him?"

"A strong possibility." She nodded several times, reminding Brynn of a chicken.

"There has to be more men in this town or nearby that read the same book."

"Romance?" June arched a brow.

"Yes. So?"

"Not many men read romance around these parts."

The very man they spoke about entered the library. "Ladies, I've some books to return."

"You're a fast reader, Mr. Brown." Brynn studied his face. Could it be him?

"Not much else to do." He smiled. "I spend the evenings alone in the hotel. Don't care much for television, so reading it is." He glanced at June. "Ma'am."

"Hmph. Why do you live at the hotel?"

"It's comfortable and no upkeep." He kept the smile on his face.

"What's your business in our town?"

"I'm actually looking for some property to invest in."

"Not much available right now." She crossed her thin arms.

Brynn cleared her throat. "You'll have to excuse my friend. She's kind of an eccentric figure in Misty Hollow." She nudged the older woman's foot in an effort to get her to stop asking so many questions.

"All right." June pressed to her feet. "I'd best be getting home where it's warm. Might rain this afternoon. Have a good day, Mr. Brown. Mind what I said, Brynlee."

"I will. Be careful. Are you driving?"

"No, my grandson is waiting in the car for me." She grinned and limped out the door.

"She's quite the character, isn't she?" David handed her the books, then stared in the direction June had gone.

"You have no idea. She's a real sweetheart. Nosy, but kind." She checked the books in. "Do you plan on checking anymore out?"

When he turned back to her, his eyes no longer held a friendly glint. Instead, they seemed hard, cold. "No, I'll be gone for a while." He flashed a smile that didn't meet his eyes and hurried from the library.

Brynn picked up the phone and called the sheriff's office.

"Deputy Hudson."

"It's Brynlee. I think I know who my stalker is, and I think he's going after June Mayfield."

"Hold on. What makes you think so?"

She told him of her conversation with June. "David rushed out of here after June grilled him about his purpose in town."

"I'll drive over there myself and make sure she's

okay."

"Thank you." Brynn hung up and grabbed her coat. The rumble of motorcycles outside let her know her ride had arrived.

~

Weston grabbed the morning's garbage and headed out the back to the dumpster. He tossed the bag inside and turned. "You have to be kidding me!"

His truck sat on the rims, all four tires slashed. A white sheet of paper flapped from under the windshield wipers.

Grabbing the paper, he marched back into the diner and locked the door. "My turn." He waved it at Lucy.

She clutched the collar of her shirt. "Oh, Lord. How do people deal with these types of situations? I'd run screaming into the night if someone threatened me in this way."

"Good afternoon." Brynn poked her head into the kitchen. She glanced at Lucy, then him. "What happened?"

"Someone slashed my tires and left me a warning. It says that I'm a barrier to getting what he wants and must be dealt with."

Her eyes widened. "Oh, I'm so sorry. I've news of my own." She told them of her suspicions regarding David. "Think about it. He's read the same book. He's in the diner for most of his meals, so he always knows what's going on with me. He's living at the hotel on some bogus business about buying land. After June questioned him at length, he said he's leaving town for a few days."

It could be nothing, but it did sound suspicious to him.

"Jane Moreland was found dead in her car, throat slit." Angela, one of the servers barged into the kitchen. "Right outside the newspaper office, too."

"That was next on the list." Brynn's voice sounded hoarse. "Someone was murdered, then the hero receives a warning. He'll go after Maddy next."

"He doesn't know where she is." Weston pulled her into his arms.

"He'll find her. Somehow, he'll find her." She trembled.

"Come on. Lucy, call Greg. I'm taking Brynn home." He turned to leave. "Aw, No tires. Guess it's repairs first." He called Ray, then led Brynn to a chair. "Sit. Decide what to eat while I get my tires replaced. Then, I'm taking you home."

"I have work to do." She punched numbers into her cell phone. "I'm calling Maddy to warn her." A few minutes later, she took a deep breath. "Maddy and her parents are heading to Europe to spend the New Year with her sister. He won't be able to get to her."

Who would he substitute? Weston stepped outside to greet Ray who had arrived with four new tires.

"These bad guys coming to town sure keep my business hopping," the mechanic said. "From wrecked cars to slashed tires, I barely know what end is up."

"Thanks for coming on such short notice."

"Not a problem. You can fetch me one of your famous burgers." The man laughed. "I'm on my lunch break."

"I'll fix that right now." Weston rushed to fix his order. He cast a quick glance at the serious expression on Brynn's face. "I'd say yes to him right now if I knew who he was. This going through the entire book is ridiculous. He's like a child playing some stupid game."

"If the perp is David Brown, and he's skipped town, maybe he left information at the hotel so they wouldn't release his room."

"We need to ask questions of your neighbors and the hotel staff. The library may have to stay closed for a day or two while we figure this out."

"Not a chance. The town relies on me being there." She shook her head.

Weston flipped the burger. "The town wants you safe first and foremost."

"I can't stay locked in the house."

"We won't be. We'll be out pounding the pavement with a motorcycle-gang escort." He grinned.

She gave a sad smile back. "We'll be perfectly safe then."

"You bet. No one will come near you." He was another story. All he could do was pray the men wanting to guard Brynn would also have his back. Weston packed Ray's lunch and rejoined him outside where a fine mist of rain had started. Four new tires replaced the bad ones. "Just in time." He handed the man his lunch. "No charge. I'll be by later to pay the bill for the tires."

"Whenever." Ray smiled. "I know where you work. Thanks for the food."

Weston gave a nod and returned to the kitchen. "We're set to go."

Brynn pushed to her feet. "I think you need to take your warning to the sheriff before we start pounding the pavement."

"Asking questions might have to wait until tomorrow. It's raining."

"Greg is coming in to cover your shift," Lucy said. "Don't worry about a thing here."

Good. He had enough to worry about. Weston held out his hand to Brynn. "Let's go find some answers." The vulnerable look in her eyes ripped at his heart. He couldn't lose her. Not when his heart had started to heal after the loss of Sybil. Why had he let down his guard and fallen in love again?

Chapter Twelve

Brynn needed to find a way to persuade Weston to leave. To move out of her house. If he were to die because of a need to protect her, she'd never get over it. It was time to put distance between them, something she should have done from the beginning.

Her heart lurched. She liked seeing him first thing in the morning, and she enjoyed his cooking for her. Putting distance between them meant no diner for a while. Tears pricked her eyes.

The rumble of motorcycles sounded, drawing her attention behind them. A long of bikes driving side by side followed. Their very own cavalry.

Weston reached for her hand. "They're a formidable sight."

She pulled away so he couldn't touch her. "Yes, they are."

Surprise flickered in his eyes. "You okay?"

"I'm fine." She stared out the window at a total loss as to how to convince him away from her without hurting him. Maybe she couldn't. Most likely the best she could hope for was to keep him at arm's distance until this was all over and pray he didn't die because of her. The book had a hero, and David Brown had designated Weston as the one. She released a sigh in a huff, steaming a small circle on the window.

"Are you upset about not returning to work?" Weston pulled into her driveway. "It's for your safety, you know."

"I know." She shoved her door open, not giving him the chance to open it for her.

"Have I done something to make you mad?" He frowned.

"Not at all. Let's start knocking on doors." She told the bikers to stay put but keep them in their sights. The roar of their engines filled the air and gave her the start of what promised to be one doozy of a headache.

"Fine." Weston grabbed her hand and marched down the sidewalk.

Leave it to her to make him upset. A muscle ticked in his jaw. His boots slapped the pavement. He knocked loudly on her neighbor's door. A dog barked from inside.

"No need to knock the door down." Mr. Farley glared. "What's so urgent?"

"My apologies." Weston took a few deep breaths which made Brynn feel worse at the sight of him trying to overcome his emotions. "Did you happen to see who decorated Brynlee's porch the other night?"

He glanced toward her house. "I thought it was you out there. Struck me as strange since it was after midnight, but to each their own."

"What made you think it was Weston?" Brynlee slipped her hand from Weston's.

"What other man would be over there except your boyfriend?"

"He isn't my boyfriend. Can you describe the

man?"

"Same build, but it was dark, so that's all I've got." He glanced from her to Weston and back. "Are you in trouble, Miss Brynn?"

He must be the only one in town who didn't know. "I have a secret admirer who isn't being very nice."

"That why Misty's Angels are following you around?"

"That's the first time I've heard them called that." She smiled.

He laughed. "They just named themselves. After that run-in with the gangs, they said they needed a way to distinguish themselves. See that one in the red beanie? That's my son. He's a lawyer sometimes."

"Did you see a vehicle that night?" Weston asked.

"A dark sedan of some sort. Looked fancy. I really didn't think too much about it. If Barney hadn't set up a ruckus, I never would've climbed out of bed to look out the window." A beagle peeked around his legs.

"Thank you for your time." Weston put his hand on Brynn's lower back as he did so often.

She fought the urge to pull away, not wanting to have the Misty Angels think they didn't need to step in. "If my nearest neighbor couldn't tell us anything, I doubt anyone else can."

"It doesn't hurt to try." He guided her across the street.

As they stepped onto the sidewalk, she moved a few inches to the right causing his hand to slip away. Brynn didn't trust herself when he touched her. Now that she'd made up her mind to keep a distance from him, all she could think about was how much her feelings had grown. She had to remind herself that not getting too close to Weston might save his life. But how to let David see?

She glanced up and down the street. No way would he have left town. He had to be hiding somewhere close by. In one of her neighbor's homes? Could he be holding one of them hostage? The thought made her gasp.

"What?" Weston peered into her face.

"Nothing. Just a crazy thought."

"I'm listening."

"What if David is in one of the houses on this street? He could be inside holding someone hostage."

His features grew grave. "That's a distinct possibility. We need to knock on every door."

She nodded and climbed the steps to Mrs. Rogers' house. The elderly woman opened the door wearing a floral robe. She blinked several times before recognizing Brynn.

"Oh, hello, dear. Why'd you put your decorations up so late in the year and take them down the next day? I'll never understand you young people."

"Did you see who put them up"

She shook her head. "I'm asleep by nine. They were there when I woke up."

Brynn leaned close and lowered her voice. "Are you alone?"

"Speak up, dear. I don't hear like I once did."

Confident Mrs. Rogers wasn't being held, they moved on to the next house. Weston rang the doorbell to Mr. Dickens's house, a small half-brick, half-wood structure.

After several knocks, the old man answered. "Yeah?"

Brynn went through the same questions as before. "Since it wasn't either of us, we're asking if anyone saw anything."

"Nope." The old man usually stayed to himself, but today he seemed especially surly.

Brynn lowered her voice. "Are you alone?"

"What kind of a nonsensical question is that?" He slammed the door.

She stood blinking like an owl. By the time they knocked on every house on the street and asked the same questions of every resident, it appeared her idea was wrong.

~

"Get away from the door." Peter motioned the gun toward the old man's sofa. "You did good." He grinned. Brynlee and the chef wouldn't suspect a thing.

He rose from the recliner and parted the curtains just enough to see the two of them climb into the chef's truck. Brynn rushed forward, not allowing the man to help her. Had the two had an argument?

No matter. He wouldn't veer much from the book's plot, and the book needed a hero. The chef had to fill that spot. There was no time for Peter to find someone else. The end of the book was fast approaching.

"I'm hungry. Fix me something to eat."

The old man glared at him. "Don't have much. I'm on a fixed income. It'll have to be soup."

"That's fine." He'd order a grocery delivery for the next day. Without knowing exactly how long he'd be in hiding, he needed more than soup. He also needed a disguise. "You have a computer?"

"Of course. I'm not dead." The old man shook his

head and shuffled to the kitchen tossing over his shoulder that the office was down the hall.

Peter didn't want to kill the man. It wasn't part of the plot, but if Mr. Dickens kept getting on Peter's nerves, he might not be able to help himself.

He headed to the office and sat in front of a carved cherrywood desk. The office didn't look as if it belonged in this simple house of meager furnishings. Full bookcases covered two walls. The leather chair he sat on barely made a sound from his weight. Peter smiled. He really did like fine things.

Thankfully, the computer didn't need a password. From the man's online history, packages were delivered on a regular basis. Good. No one would think there was anything out of the ordinary.

Peter ordered a gray wig, a moustache, blue contacts, and men's clothing befitting of a man in his sixties. No one would suspect a round-shouldered elderly man to be Peter Drury or David Brown. Invisibility made him invincible.

~

What made Brynn grow cold toward him? He cut her a glance, his gaze locked on the soft curve of her cheek. When she didn't pivot toward him, he turned the key in the ignition and pulled away from the curb.

Maybe they'd find out something at the hotel, but he doubted it. However, this man wasn't a ghost. Sooner or later, he'd make a mistake.

"If David isn't hiding at one of the neighbors' houses, where else could he hide in this town and keep an eye on you?"

She shrugged. "To watch my house, it has to be a place on my street. We checked those. If we would've had a picture of him, someone might have seen him without realizing they were looking at an insane person."

"Brown's new to town. He'd have stuck out like a sore thumb." Same as Weston had.

She shrugged again and kept staring out the window. They didn't speak again until they reached the hotel. "I bet there's a guest list to that party I went to. We could mark off all the names of people I know. I bet he's using an alias, though. How could we find out his real name?"

"I have no idea." He started to put his hand on her back, but she moved too fast for him. Something sharp stabbed his heart. "I'm sure the sheriff has already dug into the name, David Brown, and found nothing."

Inside, they approached the concierge's desk and asked to see David Brown.

"I'm sorry, but Mr. Brown has left on business."

"Did he give up his room?" Weston tried to catch a glimpse of the room number on the man's computer screen.

"No, he did not." He moved the screen so Weston couldn't see. "Sir, we value our guests' privacy."

"Did he say when he would return?"

"He did not. As long as he pays for the room, we don't care. Anything else I can help you with?"

"Do you have a guest list from the Christmas party?" Brynn smiled. "I attended and met someone I knew a long time ago, but she's remarried. I'd like to reconnect with her."

"That I can help you with." The man returned her smile and printed off the guest list. "Anything else?"

Weston shook his head. "Thank you for your

time." He led Brynn back outside. "That was a waste of time."

"We have the list." She stood under the hotel awning and scanned the names. "No David Brown on here. Do you think he could've crashed the party?"

"Did anyone check invites at the door?"

"No. We were able to simply walk in."

"Then, yeah. I think he crashed the party. Men on business trips do that all the time. Crash parties and weddings. Anything to break up the boredom." He opened the passenger-side truck door. "Back to your place or the diner?"

She pursed her lips. "The diner, I suppose. It's almost suppertime."

"How about I cook for the two of us? It's been a long day." And he wanted to find out what he'd done to upset her.

She thought for a moment, then gave a reluctant nod. "I am tired."

"Great. I'll make lasagna, salad, and garlic bread." They made a quick trip to the grocery store before heading to her place.

Hoping to catch her off guard with his question, he waited until she seemed relaxed as she prepared the salad. "What did I do for you to act as if you'd rather me not be around?"

She jerked her head up. "Nothing."

"Then what's wrong?" He removed the steaming lasagna from the oven. "I'd really like to know."

Tears filled her eyes. "The longer you remain in my company, the greater the danger to you. I couldn't bear you to suffer the same fate as the hero in the book."

He'd read the last few chapters and knew about the character almost dying in a fire. "I'm a fireman, sweetheart. That won't happen to me."

He hoped.

Chapter Thirteen

Peter strolled Main Street in his disguise, smiling and nodding at folks he passed by. He wore a peaky hat and pulled the collar of his wool coat high on his neck. Shoving his hands into the pockets of the tweed pants, he kept his shoulders hunched. Not even his mother could recognize him.

A bell jingled when he opened the door to the local pawn shop. He needed a gun for the day's task and didn't want to use his own. Something he could toss that wouldn't lead to him. Today's task was his most dangerous yet.

"Hey, old-timer. What can I do for you?" A big man stood behind the counter, suspenders stretched over his hanging belly.

"I'm looking for a handgun. Nothing too fancy."

"I ain't seen you around these parts."

"Really? My grandfather owned a farm right outside of town. Know the name Wilson?"

The man bit his lower lip, his brow wrinkled in thought. "Now, that does sound familiar. Reckon you and I just haven't been in the same places."

Peter laughed. "I'm thirty years your senior. I doubt we would." He pointed to a Glock. "That's a nice one." It had better be with a price tag of $600.

"Sure, it is. Mind filling out these papers? I'll let you take the gun, but I have to do this on my end." He slid a few sheets across the counter.

Peter had counted on the pawn shop not following the letter of the law. "Absolutely." He used his alias and made up an address for Misty Hollow. With a smile, he handed the papers over and took the weapon. Time to make a statement.

He strolled back to where he'd left a rental car. Five minutes later, he sat in the parking lot of the sheriff's office and placed a call. When the sheriff stepped outside, he aimed and fired.

Sheriff Westbrook dropped and rolled, coming to his feet with a weapon in his hand. Bravo, ex-FBI man. You have skills.

Peter fired again and burned rubber speeding from the lot. In the book, the shooter didn't missed. Still, he'd left the idea that he could pretty much get to anyone he wanted. It was a solid warning to give.

~

"Someone took a shot at the sheriff!" Wilbur, a regular at the diner, burst through the front door. "He ain't hit, though."

Brynn jumped to her feet and met Weston's gaze through the kitchen window. At his questioning look, she nodded. In the book, the detective on the case had been killed. Thankfully, David had missed.

Ron, one of the bikers, rushed to her side. "Come on. We need to drop you off at the library so we can seek vengeance on who tried to kill our sheriff."

"The library is closed today."

"Good. You stay in the diner until we come back.

If you leave, make sure it's with the chef." He hurried away.

She was getting tired of being ordered around. A full day spent in the diner didn't appeal to her either. Sure, she loved reading, but for hours on end?

A few minutes later, the sheriff and Deputy Hudson entered the diner and came her way.

"In the kitchen, please." Sheriff Westbrook waved his arm.

She shoved open the swinging door. "I'm glad you didn't meet the same fate as the detective in the book."

"Me, too. It was an idiot move for me to step outside on an unconfirmed call of a homeless man in the parking lot." He shook his head. "Rookie mistake that could've gotten me killed."

"What's up?" Weston crossed his arms.

"The man who shot at me was older. Maybe in his sixties. David Brown is twenty or thirty years younger. Has he veered from the book, Brynlee?"

"No." Her head ached between her eyes. "So far, he's followed it pretty closely. Which means, he bought the gun here in town, and he'll dispose of it behind one of the shops."

"Deputy, find that gun, then pay a visit to the pawn shop, please. I'll be here having breakfast." The sheriff exited the kitchen and slid into a booth. He motioned for her to sit across from him. "Join me, Brynlee."

She sat and crossed her arms, knowing she wouldn't like what he had to say.

"You and I both know the danger to you and Weston is going to escalate. I want the two of you to take leave of your jobs and come stay with me and my wife at our place. It's secluded. You'll be safe there."

"No. Lucy is having a New Year's Eve party tomorrow night, and I've promised to help her."

"This man is good at hiding in crowds. He could come to the party and grab you before anyone knew what happened." He fixed a steely gaze on her.

"Everyone is on alert that I have a stalker. No strangers will be allowed inside that door." This wasn't something she was willing to negotiate. "I know the plot, Sheriff. He can't catch me unawares like the heroine in the book was."

"This man is clever. He'll find a way. More people will die before this is over. Are you willing to risk that it might be you or Weston? Lucy or Greg? One of your neighbors?"

She told him how she and Weston had questioned neighbors and the hotel concierge. "Here's the list. No David Brown."

He exhaled heavily. "Stop investigating, Brynlee. You're in enough danger as it is."

"And the department needs help to stop this as soon as possible." She hiked her chin. "I feel better being an active participant in bringing this guy down. I've read plenty of crime books—"

"Do not tell me that qualifies you. You are not that stupid." He glanced over to where the deputy entered and strode toward them.

"Found the weapon behind the drugstore lying there where anyone could pick it up. I questioned the pawnshop owner, and he said he sold that gun this morning to an old man named David Brown."

The sheriff rubbed his hands roughly down his face. "He's wearing a disguise. There's no point in looking for this old man. He'll have changed to something else by now. Start knocking on doors, Deputy. He's hiding somewhere right in front of our faces."

~

Weston listened as Brynn told him what the sheriff had suggested. "I kind of agree with him—" He held up a hand to stop her protest. "But I'm also with you. I don't want to take time off my job. It's safe at the diner. You have bodyguards at the library only a fool would try and get through. We stay vigilant, and we stay safe."

"Thank you. The sheriff won't catch him if we're in hiding. He has to think he can get to me."

The very idea of David Brown getting his hands on Brynn turned his heart to ice. Not wanting to think any more on what could happen, he grabbed the garbage and headed for the dumpster out back. After tossing it inside, he leaned against the brick of the building. There were no other cars parked there but his truck.

A homeless man wandered by, stopping to stare at Weston before moving on. Could that man have been Brown? How many disguises did the man have? Every new face in Misty Hollow was suspect.

He pushed away from the building and returned to the kitchen, locking the back door. Something Lucy said they'd never had to do before the new hotel had been built.

He studied the faces in the diner, not seeing anyone new or David Brown. It galled him that the man they'd been looking for had been with them all that time, even visiting the library daily. Cutting Weston's brake line, then pretending to be the Good Samaritan. His hands curled into fists as he envisioned one of them connecting with Brown's face.

"Relax." Brynn smiled up at him. "At least you're working, not sitting here useless until it's time to go home."

"I'm sorry."

"Why? This isn't your fault. You aren't the one who went to a Christmas party, got spooked and ran, luring a stalker into our midst."

"It isn't your fault either."

"I know." She sighed and glanced at the notepad she'd picked up somewhere. "I'm occupying my time trying to figure out where he's holed up. I keep going back to a neighbor's house."

"That would mean one of them lied under duress."

"Yes." She lifted a tortured gaze. "An innocent person who might not survive this."

"Hopefully, Deputy Hudson will discover which resident he's holding." He put a hand on her shoulder, grateful she didn't pull away this time. God willing, they'd be able to explore the growing feelings they had for each other when this was all said and done.

Weston had heard that relationships formed under intense situations didn't last. He hoped theirs would be an exception.

Back in the kitchen, he stirred a large pot of broccoli-cheese soup, the lunch special for the day. Some regulars ate whatever the special was for each meal, so he always tried to make sure to have enough.

Waiting for the attack that would surely come made it hard for him to concentrate, and he burned a batch of biscuits. With a groan, he dumped them in the trash and made another batch.

"I think I have it." Brynn entered the kitchen. "I've known my neighbors for a long time. The only one who seemed even the slightest bit out of character was Mr. Dickens. He's cranky but never rude."

"Let the sheriff know. They might be able to pull some information out of the man." He hoped so without anyone getting killed.

She made the call, then returned to her table. "Now to find something else to do to fill the afternoon hours."

"Why don't you bus tables?" Lucy suggested. "I'm down a busboy today. There are extra aprons hanging in the storage room. You can keep whatever tips you make."

"Okay." She went to the back room and grabbed a plain white apron. "I've never bused tables before, but clearing dirty dishes and wiping down the tables shouldn't be hard."

"You can handle it." Weston smiled as she hurried past. His attention was drawn to two squad cars speeding past the diner, lights flashing and sirens wailing.

"They're headed to my side of town," Brynn said.

"Maybe your hunch was right." He wiped his hands and joined her at the window.

"Wish we could go see."

"Well, we can't. I'm working, and it's too dangerous. The sheriff can handle whatever it is." Everything in him wanted to follow the sheriff.

Conversations in the diner increased in volume as everyone added their own version of what could be going on.

"I'm not staying here." Wilbur slapped money on the counter. "I'll be back to fill y'all in."

"Make sure you do," Lucy called out. "Don't leave us hanging until tomorrow."

He raised a hand to let her know he'd heard.

An hour later, he returned to curious faces. Weston grinned. No one wanted to be left out of the news.

Wilbur puffed out his chest. "Seems that stalker guy was staying in Dickens' house. Eating his food, using his computer. When the authorities showed up, the stalker darted out the back door and into the woods. He's gone."

For the moment.

Chapter Fourteen

Brynn started to reach for the cranberry-colored dress she'd worn to the Christmas party. No, she doubted she'd ever wear that dress again. Instead, she pulled a simple black sheath from the closet. Her familiar fallback item when she had nothing to wear.

With her mother's pearls, the dress would be fitting for the New Year's Eve party. She held it up in front of her as she stared into the mirror. The dress always complemented her fair skin. She'd wear her hair up and put on a light touch of makeup.

From down the hall came singing. She stood still and listened. Had Weston always sung in the shower?

She peered out of her room to see the bathroom door open a couple of inches. Maybe he had, and she hadn't heard. She smiled at his soft baritone, then closed her door to get dressed.

When she exited her room, Weston came out of the bathroom. Hair wet, towel hung low on his hips…she froze, her eyes widening. She forgot what she was going to do. Her mouth felt full of cotton.

He grinned. "I'll be ready in a bit. The bathroom is all yours."

She nodded, then scurried in to do her hair and

makeup. She'd seen a man's naked chest before. Why act like a silly girl? Because, despite her resolve not to, she was falling hard for Weston Hoover.

Leaning on the sink, she let out a long, slow breath. Composure regained, she fixed her hair and put on her makeup before spritzing on a bit of perfume.

Weston whistled when she joined him in the living room. "You clean up good."

"So do you." He made black slacks and a royal blue button-up shirt look like a tuxedo. She could almost forget someone wanted to hurt her. Since there weren't any parties in the book, she felt relatively safe. In the novel, the killer lay low for a while. She hoped that was the case with her stalker.

They drove to the diner accompanied by the Misty Angels. She'd grown familiar to the growl of their bikes. Someday, she'd miss them following her everywhere she went.

"Come on in." She waved to the bikers as she climbed out of Weston's truck.

"No, ma'am. That party is too fancy for us. We'll see you after midnight." The leader led them down the street as more vehicles pulled into the parking lot.

Weston held the door open for her, then took her coat. A strand of white lights around the room provided a festive ambiance to the dimly lit diner. The counter held a bounty of finger foods prepared earlier that day by both chefs. Champagne bottles chilled in a bucket of ice. Music played from the jukebox. The center of the room had been cleared to provide space for dancing.

She glanced up at Weston. Would they dance? What would happen when the clock struck midnight?

He waved at the sheriff and his wife, Karlie. His

fingers entwined with Brynn's as they strolled the perimeter of the room, smiling and making small talk. She studied the face of everyone, relaxing when she didn't see anyone new. The party was invitation only. David Brown would not have been given one, even before they knew he was her stalker. Tonight was for Lucy's friends.

Lucy stood next to Greg, looking stunning in a black dress of her own that set off her Lucy Ricardo red hair. From the way she gazed at the older chef, there might be a romance brewing.

Weston led her to a booth near the kitchen. "Hungry?"

"A little." She set her clutch on the table and followed him to the buffet. "You and Greg outdid yourselves. This looks pretty fancy."

"It was nice to make some of the recipes I've used before." He handed her a plate. "Something other than good ole down-home recipes."

"But we all like your down-home food." She grinned and filled her plate. "It isn't often we get salmon-anything in Misty Hollow."

"Pays to have connections."

Brynn stopped halfway through the buffet line. "Why do you keep yourself between me and the window? David isn't going to try anything tonight."

"He could veer from the plot." He set a cranberry tart on her plate. "Eventually, when he doesn't succeed at getting to us, he'll have to."

"But he hasn't done everything yet. Relax and enjoy the evening."

"Oh, I will." His eyes sparkled. "I plan on dancing with you until that clock strikes twelve." The spark was replaced with a warmth so intense it sent her stomach flopping. "Then, I'm going to kiss you." He cupped her cheek with his free hand. "Will you let me?"

She nodded, once again at a loss for words.

"You're holding up the line." Sheriff Westbrook chuckled. "Move it along, or my wife will become hangry."

"My apologies." Weston laughed and ushered Brynn ahead.

Plates full, they returned to their seats. Weston sat facing the door and front window.

Brynn sighed and picked up the salmon canape. His insistence on being on guard during a time when they should be having fun irritated her. Why couldn't she have one normal day with Weston? One day to explore her growing feelings? She glanced at the window.

If she ever saw David again, she'd wring his neck.

~

It should be Peter sitting across from her. It should be him who kissed her at midnight.

She'd worn her hair up, exposing the gracefulness of her neck, the softness of her cheek. The dress hugged her in all the right places, making any sane man mad to possess her.

Peter lowered the binoculars and shivered. On top of the building across the street, a cold wind blew. He'd need a thicker coat for the winter in Misty Hollow. Unless he moved things along at a quicker pace.

In the book, the antagonist stayed low for three weeks. The hero and heroine let down their guard enough for him to fulfill his quest. What if Peter didn't wait three weeks? Brynlee and the chef would be expecting him to. Moving ahead would throw them off guard.

He lifted the binoculars again and cursed as Hoover stood and offered his hand to Brynlee. He swept her onto the makeshift dance floor and swayed to a slow song. That should be Peter breathing deeply of her scent as he held her in his arms.

Someday, it would be him. And tonight, he'd make sure there were fireworks.

~

Weston breathed deeply of the intoxicating perfume Brynn wore. He rested his cheek against her soft one. She fit perfectly in his arms. He sang along with the song, his lips near her ear.

"You have a good voice," she murmured.

He smiled and kept singing. Holding her, he gave up fighting not to care for her. Weston had lost that battle the moment he spotted the frightened gal in the park. He'd do everything in his power not to lose her as he had Sybil. Even if it meant sacrificing his life for hers.

When the song ended, they returned to the booth. Weston kept hold of her hand across the table. "You look beautiful tonight."

She gave a soft laugh. "As opposed to other nights?"

"You're always beautiful." He lifted her hand to his lips.

"Could you help me in the kitchen?" Greg's head nodded in that direction.

"Sure." He reluctantly released Brynn's hand with promises to return as soon as possible.

"Smell anything?"

Weston sniffed. "Gas?"

"Yeah and look at this." He stepped out the back door that led to the short hallway with access to the storeroom and the back exit. "The locks have been broken. Someone probably used the sound of the music to cover the noise of breaking them. I need you to help me make sure the perp isn't hiding somewhere in the diner."

Weston nodded, his blood boiling. "I'll check the restrooms. You check the storage room and the freezer." Couldn't he have one night with Brynn without this psycho ruining everything?

He pushed open the women's restroom. "Anyone in here?" When no one answered, he entered and peered under each of the stalls. Empty. He did the same with the men's room. Finding it empty, he peered out the back door, glancing this way and that, fully expecting a bullet to ring out.

"What's going on?"

He spun around to face the sheriff. "Someone broke in through the back door and turned on the gas in the kitchen."

"We need to get everyone out." The sheriff glanced at his watch.

"Hold on." Greg stepped out of the storage room. "Here's what we're smelling." He held up a can of skunk spray. "A prank."

"The broken lock is no prank." Sheriff Westbrook shook his head. "The perp has a plan. He wouldn't break in, then leave without expecting a reaction. Where's Brynlee?"

"In the booth."

"Don't leave her. Keep your eyes open. He's going

to try something." The sheriff took the can of spray and strode back to the dining section.

Weston rejoined Brynn and filled her in on what happened.

"Why would he use prank spray?" Her brow furrowed. "That's something a teen would do. They use fart spray—pardon my language—in the library all the time."

"I'm sure we'll find out before the night is over." He glanced at the front window again feeling exposed.

"I'm sorry," she said.

"For what?" He put his hand over her folded ones. "You can't possibly believe this is your fault."

"It is me he's infatuated with. Me he wants to possess. You simply got in the way that evening in the park."

He smirked. "Every story needs a hero. If not me, then someone else. I'm a firefighter, remember?"

"A true hero indeed." She gave a sad smile. "This has put a damper on the festivities. Same as it did at Christmas."

"I'll make you forget about it all when I kiss you." He glanced at the clock. "Not long now."

Her cheeks turned a lovely shade of pink. "Pretty sure of yourself, aren't you?"

"Yes, ma'am. I've been told I'm a great kisser."

Her brows rose. "Kissed a lot of women, have you?"

"My fair share." A dimple winked in his cheek. "I have to start pouring Champagne. Want to help?"

"Sure." She slid from the booth and followed him to the buckets of ice and single-size bottles of bubbly.

"We thought these would be easier than handing

out flutes and pouring."

"Less clean up, that's for sure."

Together they handed everyone in the diner a bottle, then clustered in the center of the room as midnight approached. Someone put another slow song on the jukebox—a song that should carry them right up to midnight.

Weston pulled Brynn into his arms, resting his chin on top of her head. Whatever would come, they had this moment. A perfect moment swaying to the music, holding her. He closed his eyes, snapping them open when the song ended, and the countdown began.

"Ten, nine, eight…" Voices rang out.

Keeping his arm around Brynn's waist, he joined in the countdown. When "Happy New Year" burst from everyone's lips, he lowered his and kissed her.

Chapter Fifteen

Weston was right. He was a terrific kisser. As the kiss deepened, Brynn's arms wrapped around his neck.

Champagne bottles popped around them. She stepped back and smiled up at him as he opened her bottle. "At least you delivered."

His laugh filled her heart. Then, his eyes opened wide, and he paled. "Don't spray that!"

A woman picked up a can from the sheriff's table and sprayed.

Someone shouted, "Gas leak!"

Pandemonium broke out as everyone raced for the front doors.

"Stop." Sheriff Westbrook tried to block them but was soon knocked out of the way. "Don't go out there."

Brynn clutched Weston's arm. "What's happening?"

"Sheer panic. Stay down." He shoved her under a booth as a shot rang out.

Someone screamed, then another shot and another.

Brynn put her hands over her ears and trembled. He'd lured people out in a sniper shooting. "This isn't in the book." She shook her head. "He's veering away from the plot. We have no idea what he's going to do next."

"Don't panic. We'll figure this out." Weston's gaze locked with hers. "If you lose control, he wins."

"Karlie!" The sheriff rushed back into the diner.

"I'm here." His wife waved at him from under a table.

A shot spun the sheriff in a circle. He dropped and crawled to his wife, leaving a trail of blood behind him.

"I need to check on him." Weston cupped Brynn's face. "It's my job."

She nodded, her stomach in knots. Outside, screams filled the air, but the shots had stopped. People would need help. She started to crawl from under the table.

"Not yet." Weston barked. "We have to make sure he's gone. Stay put."

She crawled to where he worked on the sheriff. Blood pooled from the other man's shoulder. "You need something to stop the bleeding." Staying low, she darted to the kitchen and grabbed several clean rags and an apron. She shoved them at Weston. "You can use the apron strings to tie the rags in place. Anything else?"

A gleam of appreciation shone in his eyes. "You sure aren't that same woman who fainted in this diner when you saw me."

"I told you I hadn't eaten that morning." She'd never live that down.

"The bullet caught me in the shoulder." The sheriff ground through his teeth. "Karlie can care for me. The two of you are needed outside. The shooter made his point. I'm sure he's gone, but just in case, stay together. He doesn't want either of you dead yet."

"This isn't part of the book," Brynn said. "We don't know what he'll do."

"I'm sorry." The woman who had sprayed the can crawled from under a table. "I thought it was a noisemaker."

Which is what the man had counted on, most likely. "It's okay." Brynn forced a smile. "Find your husband."

Lucy and Greg came from behind the lunch counter. "I'll grab more rags to help with those outside," Lucy said. "The first responders are going to need all the help they can get."

Weston stood and helped Brynn to her feet. "Let's go. Prepare yourself. It won't be pretty."

"I'm fine." She hoped as she grabbed her coat.

They stepped into a war zone. Car windows had been shattered. People groaned from behind the vehicles. Several lay in the parking lot, not moving.

"We need to see which of the wounded are the worst so the first responders can work on them before the less wounded. The dead will have to wait." Weston's voice sounded chilled, detached.

She took an armful of rags from Lucy and followed Weston. He knelt next to the drugstore owner, Mr. Smithson. The man had been shot twice. Once in the thigh, the other in the side.

"I'm fine," he said. "Move on to someone worse."

"We need to stop the bleeding." Brynn knelt beside him, drawing strength from Weston, and pressed a rag to his side. "I've got him, if you want to check on someone else."

Weston nodded. "Stay where I can see you."

"That goes for you, too." While Weston was

preoccupied, it would be the perfect time for David to take him. Her gaze locked for a second on his retreating back. She wanted him to stay with her.

She tore an apron string off and tied it around Mr. Smithson's waist, then did the same for his leg. "The paramedics will be here soon. Where is your wife?"

"I don't know. We got separated."

She patted his shoulder. "I'll try to find her." She prayed she wouldn't find her dead.

The woman was slumped against the wall of the building. She'd been shot in the stomach but still breathed. "Weston!" She didn't have a clue what to do for a gut shot.

He hurried toward her. "Ah, this isn't good." He pressed a rag to the woman's stomach. "You'll have to hold this tight. Press hard. Don't stop, even if she comes to. The paramedics are almost here."

Sirens wailed, splitting the sounds of cries and groaning as two ambulances pulled into the parking lot. It wasn't enough. They needed more. None of those who had fled from the diner had escaped injury. Only those now trickling through the door had escaped.

"Brynlee." A loud whisper came from around the corner of the building. "I'm here."

Her heart raced. She glanced up to see David staring around the corner. "Why?"

"It's all a game, isn't it, darling? These people are simply collateral damage." He tilted his head. "You see me now, don't you?"

"Yes." The word came out like a gasp. "What do you want?"

"Call your hero."

She took a deep breath. "No."

"I will rid you of him, so that I am the only hero in your life."

"You are no hero," she snarled, keeping pressure on Mrs. Smithson's wound. "You're a murderer. You're insane."

His features hardened. "Until you realize that you belong to me, this type of destruction will continue. I will have you, Brynlee. You were mine the moment I laid eyes on you and saw you smile." His gaze jerked up, and he melted back into the shadows.

~

"I've done my best to assess the injuries." Weston walked beside the paramedic. "The dead are over here. The more severely wounded over there, and those with minor wounds are here." He pointed to each section of the parking lot.

"You did this yourself?"

"Those who could move went where I asked them to. The others I helped." Exhaustion weighed on his shoulders. Blood stained his clothes and caked his hands.

"We'll take it from here, Hoover. You did good." He clapped Weston on the shoulder. "It's great to have you on our team."

Weston nodded. "I've a woman over here in bad shape." He led the paramedic to where he'd left Brynn. "She's alive, but not doing well at all."

"Got it. You can step aside now, ma'am."

Brynn rose to shaky feet. "Where's the sheriff?"

"Sitting by one of the ambulances. Why?" He put his hand on her back. "Are you okay?"

"David came up to me while I was helping Mrs. Smithson." Weston rubbed her trembling hands. "He wanted me to call for you. I wouldn't."

"That's a good thing." He drew her close. "He'd have killed me." Weston glanced around the corner of the building expecting to see David waiting for him. Relief fortified his knees when he didn't see anyone. He led Brynn to the sheriff who listened stoically as she told him.

The sheriff adjusted the sling holding his arm. "Gutsy. He's stepping up his game. And, there is no David Brown in any records that looks like this man. He's using an alias."

"This is going to get very bad very fast," Karlie said. "People were killed tonight."

"The only way to stop him is to let him take me." Weston squared his shoulders.

"No." Brynn stepped closer to him. "You can't."

"We need to set a trap, Sheriff. He needs to take me, so he can come for Brynn. That's when you have to stop him."

"Let's take care of this first. Come into the office tomorrow, and we'll discuss this further. Today, we rest and mourn. For now, I'm headed to the hospital to get stitched up." He followed his wife to her car.

"You can't." Brynn shook her head. Her hair had come loose from her updo and flew around her face. "You cannot sacrifice yourself."

"People will continue to die if I don't. I can't have that on my conscience. Let's go home, clean up, and sleep all day." He ushered her to the car while she continued to protest his decision.

"We'll run away. Let's lure him away from Misty Hollow and take him down together." She clicked her seatbelt into place.

"No." He gritted his teeth.

"I can make the same sacrifice as you." Her voice hardened. "What makes you so special?"

He narrowed his eyes. "Because I care for you, and I will not lose you like I did Sybil."

Tears shimmered in her eyes. "I don't want to lose you either. That's why I wanted you to go away. Why I didn't want to get close to you." The tears fell. "If you weren't with me, David wouldn't feel as if he needed to get rid of you."

"But, I am here, sweetheart." He wiped her tears away with the pad of his thumb. "It's too late. I'm invested in bringing him down. Don't think for one second that I plan on letting him kill me." He forced a smile. "I have a few tricks up my sleeve." He started his truck and drove them home.

Deputy Hudson waited on the porch. "The sheriff wants me to check out the house before you go in."

Weston nodded. "Thanks." He wrapped his arms around Brynn in an attempt to keep her warm as the deputy entered the house.

After what seemed like forever, the deputy returned. "All clear. The back door and the windows are locked. Make sure you lock this one. Call if trouble arrives. I'll do regular drive-bys."

"We appreciate it." Weston hurried Brynn inside and locked the door. "Go shower. I can wait." He headed for the kitchen sink needing more than anything to wash off the blood.

While it had been nice for the deputy to check the house, Weston knew that David could get in. He had before. Once his hands were clean, he searched the house for a weapon. Any type of weapon.

He found a yardstick and jammed that into the sliding-glass door. It wouldn't be too hard to break, but it would alert them to someone trying to come in. He placed a kitchen chair under the front doorknob.

Knowing Brynn wouldn't use the butcher knife he'd found, he removed the bottom portion of the broom. "Keep this by your bed in case David breaks in. Don't hesitate to hit him." It wouldn't stop him for long. All Weston needed was for her to provide him with the time he needed to come to her aid.

"What about you?"

"I have this." He held up the knife. "Wish I had a gun."

"I have one." She turned and darted to her bedroom. "It belongs to my father." She reached to the top shelf of her closet and removed a metal box. "He insisted I keep it while he and my mother travel."

"Why haven't you brought it out before?"

She shrugged. "I don't really know how to use it. Do you?"

"Of course." He smiled. Having the weapon would even the playing field a bit. "Do you have anything else?"

"Pepper spray in my nightstand. Mom's suggestion for self-protection."

"Keep it on you."

She nodded. "I never thought I'd have anything to worry about."

He rested his forehead against hers. "Unfortunately, we have a lot to worry about, but these weapons will help us. I'm going to shower now. Good night."

"Good night."

After his shower, Weston took one more walk through the house. He peered through the front-window blinds. Was that someone standing between the two houses across the street? When he looked again, no one stood there.

Chapter Sixteen

Two days later, a disgruntled Brynn followed Weston into the sheriff's office. The last thing she wanted to do was make a plan to lure out her stalker using Weston as bait. How much help could the sheriff be with his arm in a sling? Would Brynn be able to save Weston if it came down to it?

"You've been out of sorts for two days." Weston opened the door. "Don't you want this to end?"

"Yes, but not at your expense." She marched past him.

"I don't plan on letting that psycho kill me. He'll try, but don't give up on me yet."

She wanted to believe everything would turn out fine. That they'd both be safe and could explore a relationship together, but fear choked her as effectively as if David Brown had his hands wrapped around her neck.

Her hands shook as she took a seat at the conference table where the sheriff and two deputies already sat. Then, she jumped up and grabbed water bottles for everyone off the sideboard before sitting down again.

Sheriff Westbrook watched with an amused gleam

in his eye. "Nervous?"

"Shouldn't I be?"

"I'm calling in the FBI so we'll have some help. After the carnage of New Year's Eve, we definitely can't do this on our own. Ah." He stood as two men and one woman dressed in black suits entered the room. "Agents White, Snowe, and Larson. Welcome. This is Brynlee Bourge and Weston Hoover."

The agents nodded and took their seats. "We were able to get a partial fingerprint off the side of the building where Miss Bourge said the perp spoke with her. It was enough to make a positive ID. The man we're looking for is Peter Drury," Agent Snowe said.

"Of Drury Shipping?" The sheriff frowned. "Are you sure?"

"Positive."

"Who is he?" Brynn glanced from one man to the next.

"Simply one of the richest men in America," Weston said. "Why would he be doing this?"

"His former nanny said he's been suffering from mental illness for years now. Ever since his parents died in a private plane crash ten years ago. Peter stopped going into the office every day. He travels wherever the mood strikes him."

"David Brown said he was in Misty Hollow on business." Brynn twisted the cap off her bottle. Money couldn't buy everything, it seemed. At least not a stable mind.

"He probably thinks he was." Agent Snowe folded his hands on the table and fixed his dark gaze on her. "He is a very unstable man. Are we sure we want to proceed with a trap?"

"Yes." Weston held Brynn's hand. "We want this to end."

"We're going to need you, Mr. Hoover, to be outside alone on a regular basis. Working in the yard should suffice, house repairs, anything that keeps you busy so Drury can make his move. We'll put a tracker on both your phone and watch in order to locate you once he has you."

Brynn's breath hitched. "What if he makes Weston take off his watch?"

"I'll swallow the tracker."

Agent Snowe shook his head. "It'll start to dissolve and leak acid. You'll be dead in a day."

"How long do you think I'll have until he tries to kill me?"

"A day or two. No more than that. Miss Bourge will have to meet him as soon as possible after your capture. Then, we'll come in and take him down."

"You hope." Brynn barely spoke above a whisper.

"We hope. We've rented the house across the street, so we can keep an eye on what is going on."

"Mr. Dickens?"

"Yes. He alerted us to the fact that Drury was staying there but left a couple of days ago. Dickens is more than willing to let us stay there while he goes on vacation." The agent headed to the door, followed by the other two. "We'll be in touch." With a nod, he and the others left the room.

"So?" Sheriff Westbrook tilted his head.

"I'm terrified." Brynn tightened her hold on Weston's hand.

"I have to admit to a bit of nervousness myself." Weston's thumb rubbed the top of her hand. "Do I put up a fight when he comes? Go along willingly? I'm not sure how to react."

"Play it by ear. Drury will most likely threaten Brynn if you don't come willingly. If so, that's your cue." He exhaled heavily. "I'm sorry it's come to this. I really am."

~

Peter had seen the agents enter Dickens' house. The black SUV and dark suits gave them away.

His attention turned to Brynn's place where Hoover followed her up the steps and into the house. He'd have to make his move soon. Things were becoming too hot for him to dawdle. He'd been enjoying the game, but all good things had to come to an end.

The lovely Brynlee wouldn't come unless he baited her with Hoover. Taking the chef wouldn't be easy with agents living across the street. He'd have to find a way of getting to him when he wasn't at the house.

Peter drummed his fingers on the steering wheel. The diner would be the best place if he could enter from the back unseen. Hoover always went in early. Of course, he always had Brynlee with him. He could take them both, but that hadn't been his plan.

Hmm. The original plan was to claim Brynlee for his own. What if he left the chef out of the game and went straight for the prize? She'd be easier to nab at the diner than the chef would be. Once Hoover was in the kitchen, Peter could simply enter the building and take her.

An elderly woman walking her dog slowed and peered into his car. Nosy neighbors. He smiled and gave a friendly nod before pulling away from the curb.

After a few days of watching, he'd know Hoover's schedule. He couldn't proceed on his new plan with Lucy and the other chef there. Too many cooks spoiled the soup.

~

"The funeral for those the town lost is tomorrow." Weston pulled a pork loin from the oven. "They decided to do all four of them at once."

"The townspeople are close." Brynn set the table. "It makes sense to attend one large funeral rather than four smaller ones. Do you think Peter will show?"

He shrugged. "They always seem to in the movies. I wish he was still following the book. At least we'd have some idea of what's next." Weston set their supper on the table and sat across from Brynn. "It'll be over soon."

She nodded, keeping her head down. "I know."

"What's wrong?"

She raised tear-filled eyes. "One of us, or both, might not be around when it's over."

"But the killing of townspeople will end." He'd do everything in his power to make sure Brynlee made it out alive. After they ate, he washed dishes and she dried. Communication was sparse, both of them knowing that he would start his outside "chores" that evening.

"Where do you think Peter is hiding?" Brynlee dried a plate.

"You know the area better than I do. I'm guessing it would be close by."

She nodded and put the plate in the cupboard. "There aren't any empty houses near here, although there are a lot of empty stores over on West Street, but it would be too cold for him to hole up there. Maybe in another neighbor's house?"

"After the shooting, I doubt anyone would stay quiet even at the risk of their life if he tried to push his way in."

"He won't have gone back to the hotel. There's a motel on the Interstate. If he's wearing a good enough disguise, he might be able to get a room there."

That would be Weston's guess. After all, the man knew about disguises. Otherwise, someone would have seen him by now. He sent the sheriff a text and received a reply that the FBI had already checked the motel. They had no other option but to wait.

After the dishes were finished and put away, Weston donned his coat and stepped into the frigid winter night. There weren't many repairs that needed to be done around the place. Brynn's father had kept the house well-maintained, but he'd have to find something to pretend to be busy with. Weston opened the small shed behind the house and pulled out a rake. He'd sweep the few leaves remaining on the ground. As he worked, he kept his eyes alert for anyone lurking in the shadows of the neighboring houses. Like the night before when he thought he saw something and blinked only to find it gone. *My imagination is working overtime.*

After raking, he took a hammer and nails and checked the shutters around the front windows. A chilly wind had picked up, making working outside unpleasant. How long was he expected to stay outside?

After an hour of pretending to be busy, he entered the house and set the board in place and a kitchen chair against the door, as he would do each night. "It's too cold to do anything more. I'll go out each night after supper and piddle around like it's my new routine. Eventually, he'll come."

She pressed a button on the television remote. "They've put out an APB on Peter Drury. He wore a disguise as David Brown. Peter has one blue eye and one brown, with dark blond hair."

"Easy to spot if he's not wearing contacts." He shrugged off his coat and sat on the sofa next to her.

A knock sounded at the door. Although he didn't expect Peter to knock, Weston grabbed the handgun from the coffee table and hurried to the door. He moved the chair and opened the door slowly to show Agent Snowe standing there. "Come on in."

"Just for a minute." He stepped just inside the door, his gaze scanning the room. "The sheriff received a call from one of your neighbors who reported a suspicious car parked on the road shortly after we arrived at the Dickens' house. Seen anything?"

"No. I was outside for over an hour and saw nothing."

"Drury is close." His gaze flicked to the kitchen chair. "That ought to slow him down." His mouth twitched. "Ever considered a security system?"

"My father has, but we've never had need of one before." Brynn turned off the television.

Weston would have put one in after the gang wars that had plagued the town. "It's too late now. We want him to gain access to us."

"Keep doing what you're doing. See you at the funeral tomorrow." The agent left.

"Why couldn't he have called?" Brynn narrowed

her eyes. "Did he think we were harboring Peter? Now, if Peter was watching everything, he would've seen the agent coming here."

"I'm sure it was nothing more than to take a quick look to see how we were." They had enough worries without creating more.

"Maybe." She stood. "I'm headed to bed. Goodnight."

"Hold on." He held out his arms. "After that New Year's Eve kiss, I've been craving more."

"Really?" She arched a brow and smiled. "You haven't even tried."

"Didn't want to push my luck, but a man can only take so much." He tilted her face to meet her eyes. "We will get through this, Brynn."

"Promise?"

"I promise." Weston prayed he hadn't just lied to her. He lowered his head and claimed her lips, wanting as much of her as he could get in whatever time they had left. If they did make it out alive, he'd spend the rest of his life making sure the woman in his arms never worried about danger again.

Chapter Seventeen

Brynn dressed in black slacks and a white and black sweater. She stared at her pale face in the mirror, relieved that neither she nor Weston had been a victim. Somehow, Peter seemed to have known they wouldn't rush from the building as so many others had. He seemed to know them as well as a close friend or a family member would.

Weston knocked on her door. "Ready?"

"Coming," she called, pulling a black duster coat from her closet. It wasn't as warm as her wool coat, but more fitting for the day.

Weston wore black pants and a grey shirt. He helped her into her coat and stepped onto the porch before her. "Coast is clear."

They dashed to his truck and locked the doors. After turning the key in the ignition, Weston cranked on the heater, blasting them both with cold air before it warmed. "I'm not familiar with where the funeral home is."

"Over the bridge and on the left." She pulled her coat tighter around her. "I doubt we'll be able to find a parking spot. We'll have to park across the street and walk." She glanced toward Mr. Dickens' house. No

SUV in the drive.

They didn't talk during the short drive to the funeral home. Her mind dwelled on the awful night of New Year's Eve. What point had it served? Peter had asked her if she saw him now. He'd had her attention since the night of the Christmas party. Only now she had a face to put with the fear.

Weston parked behind the funeral home rather than across the street. "It's too cold."

"No argument from me." She stepped from the truck and glanced around. Nothing there but four hearses and a dumpster. Brynn followed Weston around to the front and signed her name in the four guest books that sat side by side, choking up at each one, but more so at seeing Mrs. Smithson's name. The poor woman she'd helped hadn't made it.

Weston put his arm around her shoulders and led her to a pew. Once they sat, he kept ahold of her hand.

Through her tears, she gazed on the four caskets and abundance of floral arrangements. There'd be a gathering at the diner afterward for anyone who cared to come. Lucy and Greg had started cooking early that morning saying they wanted the diner to be a place people liked to gather rather a place where a violent act had taken place.

Brynn hoped for Lucy's sake that the townspeople could get over New Year's Eve. Not to forget—no one would ever forget—but to move on, carrying their loss close to their hearts.

After the service, rather than attend the actual burial, Weston and Brynn would head to the diner to help with the final details. Brynn glanced around as she stood. The agents lined the back wall. Couldn't they have tried to blend in? She studied the faces of those around her. Maybe Peter hadn't come after all.

"How many do you think will come to the diner?" Weston asked as they parked by the diner.

"It'll be full. Southern people like to eat after a funeral."

"Weird."

"How do they do it up north?"

"Depends on your ethnic group. My Irish side throws a party and gets drunk while they tell stories about the deceased."

"Sounds morbidly fun." Brynn froze at the door to the diner. Her breathing increased. No. She would not allow anxiety to overtake her every time she entered what had once been her favorite place.

"It's okay, sweetheart." Weston prodded her forward. "I'm here."

She nodded and took another step forward. What if something bad happened again? The diner would be full of mourners. What if Peter did something? She turned to leave only to find her path blocked by not only Weston, but others who had decided not to attend the burial. If they could do this, then so could she. Brynn took a deep breath, squared her shoulders, and marched to the kitchen. "What can I do to help?"

"We're going to serve buffet-style, so these trays need to go on the lunch counter." Lucy handed her a tray of sliced ham. "We're keeping it simple today, Weston. None of that fancy-city stuff."

He laughed. "Comfort food at its finest." He picked up a tray of macaroni and cheese.

Brynn carried tray after tray to the counter, amazed it didn't collapse under the weight of the food. Those in the diner filled their plates so they could eat and leave before those who'd gone to the gravesite entered. There wouldn't be enough seats.

She peered out the front window. Peter, where are you?

~

Why hadn't they come to the gravesite? He'd planned on grabbing Brynn there when everyone's attention was on the caskets and the preacher's words.

Now, he'd need another plan. He'd never get close enough at the diner with all the people there eating and sharing their stories as they did at most wakes. He punched the trunk of the nearest tree, grazing his knuckles. Just once, he'd like things to go as planned.

The phone's buzz from his pocket startled him. Very few had the number. He pulled out the phone and stared at the screen. An alert from his bank letting him know his accounts had been closed. Only one person could do that. His former nanny. She'd need to be disposed of.

But how? The authorities would be watching the mansion in New York. Her house too, most likely. After New Year's Eve, they be checking cars on the interstate.

Peter cursed under his breath. The nanny would have to wait her turn until he'd dealt with Brynlee. But hiding out in whatever hole he could find was getting old. He'd almost frozen the night before. Time to step up his game.

~

The door to the diner opened and closed as people came and went. The family members of the deceased occupied one section and the others filed by to pay their respects.

Watching Brynn fill plates and drinks for the families warmed Weston's heart. By serving others, she'd overcome her fear of the place she'd loved so much.

He studied every face that came and went, noting that the FBI agents did the same. No one resembled Peter in the slightest, not even with a disguise. The man would be foolish to come here with so many people.

Weston checked the ice under the potato salad and refilled the offerings of the makeshift salad bar. The entire town wasn't there, but the diner still bulged at the seams. The way the community rallied around one another made him very happy to have chosen Misty Hollow as his home. His gaze landed on Brynn again. Especially after meeting her. He never thought he'd love again after Sybil. Brynn must have felt his eyes on her because she grinned at him as he made his way to the kitchen.

When he returned to the lunch counter with more ham, her smile was gone; in fact, Brynn looked visibly shaken. She clutched a sheet of paper, face pale, and stared at the door. He set the pan down and rushed to her side.

"Brynn?"

"He was here. He gave me this." She held up the paper. Scrawled across it in black was the word *Soon*.

"Come on. We can't start a panic. Let's give this to Snowe."

She trembled under his arm as they made their way through the crowd to where Snowe stood with a plate in his hand. The man's eyes narrowed as they approached, and he set the plate on the nearest table. "In the kitchen."

They followed him away from curious eyes. Brynn handed him the sheet.

"Peter came dressed as an old woman, hunched over, gray hair covered with a scarf. He didn't even lift his head; just handed me this." She leaned against the counter.

"How do you know it was him?" Snowe glanced at the word on the page.

"His cologne. It's the same he's worn every time I've seen him."

Snowe headed for the door.

"He's gone," she called after him. "Gave me the paper and left after whispering I'd better not alert anyone to his presence, or we'd have a repeat of New Year's Eve. I waited until he was gone."

"You did the right thing." Weston gathered her in his arms.

Soon. He released a long pent-up breath. Things were spiraling out of control. This guy had no conscience, no fear. A dark ending seemed to be fast approaching.

They exited the kitchen as the three agents left the diner to view the street. They wouldn't find Peter. The man was too smart to linger. He turned to Brynn. "Are you going to be able to get through the day?"

Brynn nodded. "It's the mention of New Year's Eve that rattled me. That and the way he got so close without me knowing. If I hadn't smelled his cologne, I would've thought he'd sent an old woman to deliver his message." She raised her face to his. "But it wasn't only the cologne. He stunk. Like he hadn't bathed in a while. The cologne couldn't cover the body odor. I don't think he's staying in a motel."

Weston widened his eyes and glanced back out the window. "Then where?"

"The homeless camp out by the lake."

He knocked on the window and waved for Snowe to come back in, then had Brynn tell the agent what she'd told him.

"Good job. We'll send an undercover agent out there—someone who will blend in. Don't worry, we'll find him." He stepped back outside and spoke into his phone.

"Why didn't Peter tell me to go with him? I would have. All he had to do was make the same threat, and I'd have gone without a second thought."

Weston knew that, and it scared the heck out of him. "Because he has to get rid of me first."

"There's no need to use you as bait anymore in order to get to me. This entire town is the bait." She shuddered. "He isn't making sense."

Which made him all the more dangerous. "Come sit down." He led her to an empty chair. "There's nothing more we can do but wait." Wait for Peter to get rid of Weston before running off with Brynn. By doing so, in Peter's warped mind at least, he'd have erased the one thing keeping Brynn from loving him.

Weston glanced at the worry creasing her face. Did she love him? He had no doubt she cared for him. He also knew she'd never love a murderer. That would cause Peter to snap and kill her. Weston had to get to the man before he got to Brynn. The question was how?

By leaving Brynn alone in her house. Tomorrow night, he'd sneak out and go to the homeless camp. The place shouldn't be too hard to find. He'd hunt Peter down and alert the FBI once he did. It was time to take matters into his own hand and end the man's sick game.

"What are you thinking about?" Brynn looked at him with suspicion. "You're planning something."

"Not at all." He smiled. "Just wanting this to be over and done with." He'd ask forgiveness for his lie later. "Let's start cleaning up so we can go home. Almost everyone has left."

"Fine, keep your secrets, but I'll find out eventually." She pushed to her feet and headed for the counter.

"Greg and I will clean up." Lucy waved her hands at them. "You too have done enough today. Been through enough."

"These are your people, too." Brynn shook her head.

"True, but I don't have the extra worry of a killer stalking me. Go home. Be safe." She took both of their hands. "Lean on each other."

"That's the best idea I've heard in a while." Weston grinned and held out Brynn's coat. "I'll be in for my shift in the morning."

Brynn slipped her arms into the sleeves. "I feel like I could sleep for days."

They passed the three agents on their way to his truck. The agents climbed into their SUV and followed them home before heading to their rental.

Weston paused at the front door and glanced up and down the street. The hair on the back of his neck prickled. Peter was watching from somewhere.

Chapter Eighteen

The next night, Weston stopped at Brynn's bedroom door and listened. Not hearing anything, he continued down the hall, quietly removing the chair from the front door. Stepping out, he locked the door behind him. He backed from the driveway without lights, then drove toward the lake. He'd asked Greg that morning where the camp was, so he had a good idea which direction to head.

He parked in a gravel parking lot near a park and grabbed a flashlight from the glove box before setting off through the trees. It didn't take long to see the flicker of several fires.

Tents of various sizes were lined up facing each other. Metal barrels burned wood that wouldn't do the folks much good on a frigid winter night unless they huddled around the flames. Still, it lit the place up enough for Weston to make his way in and around the tents.

A few people had chosen to make shelters out of cardboard and plywood. All of the occupants stood around the fires. He didn't blame them. He'd sleep during the day when the temps were a bit warmer.

His heart ached to see people living in such

conditions. Weston vowed to bring them all something hot to eat at the first opportunity. Food, blankets, and propane heaters with enough gas to get them through the winter. He counted over twenty "homes."

Heads turned as he passed. In such a small community, strangers were certain to be noticed. He approached one of the cans. "Mind if I join you? Wife kicked me out. I don't have anywhere else to go."

"Sure," one man said. "There's plenty of room."

"Why not sleep in your vehicle?" Another asked. "She can't stay mad long."

"She hid the keys." How easily the lies rolled off his tongue. He'd have a lot of repenting to do. "It's okay. You're right. It'll blow over soon. Do you get many newcomers out here?"

"Lately we have. One a few days ago, then another yesterday. Drifters, both of them, just passing through. Said they were only staying for a day or two. Newcomers have to sleep in one of the boxes. Those of us with tents worked hard for the luxury of canvas over our heads."

That meant if Peter was here, he'd be in one of the shoddier dwellings.

"Single women sleep over there." He motioned his head to the tents on the other side. "We try to keep them safe from riffraff."

"I'll steer clear." He grinned. "If I decide to sleep, do I choose any box that's empty?"

"Yep."

While he made idle chitchat, Weston continually studied the area around him. Was Peter here as a man or a woman? Weston couldn't very well sneak around the women's tents. The men had made it clear they were protective of the women. "Any new women?"

"Nah. Not for a while. Why are you so interested in newcomers? You a cop?" The man narrowed his eyes.

"Just curious. I didn't know this place existed until I heard someone mention it." He stomped his feet to try and warm them, noticing the others stood on cardboard or pieces of carpet. "Y'all been out here long?"

"Five years for me. I'm Shep. Arthur was the first to pitch a tent. He's been here ten years."

"The law doesn't mind?"

"The former sheriff used to give us some grief, but Sheriff Westbrook says as long as we keep things civil, we can stay." Shep shrugged.

"He's a good man." Weston glanced toward the cardboard boxes, then the other burning barrels. Peter could be standing around one of them at that very moment watching him.

"I'd like to get my hands on whoever shot him."

So would Weston. "Y'all keep up on the news from town?"

"Sure. A lot of us have jobs. We keep everyone informed. I pick up garbage around the lake. Doesn't pay much, but keeps me in beer." He laughed. "None of us have hifalutin jobs that would put a real roof over our heads, but we make do."

"I can see that. I'm going to turn in after all. Good night."

"Grab some newspaper from over there. You'll need it to cover up with."

"Thanks." Weston liked Shep. He'd definitely do what he could to make these people's lives easier.

The first box he peered into was empty. He tripped

over feet passing the second one. "Sorry, dude."

When no response came, he stopped, noticing the knife in the man's chest. He stumbled back, knocking someone to the ground. He whirled and frowned at the sight of Brynn staring up at him.

"What are you doing here?"

~

"Following you." She jumped to her feet and brushed herself off. "I knew you were up to something."

He gripped her arm and pulled her behind a tent. "There's a dead man in that box. We have to call the sheriff."

A man cried out. "Got a stiff over here! Where's that nosy guy? He killed him."

"Is he talking about you?" Brynn peered around the tent.

"Probably." Keeping a tight hold of her hand, he darted for the trees. "We'll call the sheriff from my truck."

Voices rose behind them.

"They're coming after us." Her throat seized. It sounded like a mob she'd seen on a movie once where the townspeople rallied together to bring down a killer.

"I'm not parked far from here." He clicked on his flashlight.

"They'll see that."

"We have to go to the truck. If we fall, they'll be on us."

God, help us. Her breathing came in gasps.

"Can you make it?"

"You bet." Nothing would stop her from reaching the safety of the truck. "What about my car?"

"We'll come back for it tomorrow."

They burst from the trees into the parking lot. The moment Weston pressed the button on the truck's fob, Brynn hurled herself into the passenger side seat.

Weston roared from the lot before she had her seatbelt in place. He peered in the rearview mirror. "That was close." He grinned.

"Are you enjoying yourself?" She frowned.

"Maybe. Being chased by a mob is a new experience."

"And having a killer after you isn't?" She shook her head and clicked her seatbelt into place. "Why did you lie to me about your plans?"

"I'm sorry. I didn't want you in harm's way."

"Did you actually think you'd find Peter?" She stared at his strong profile.

"Yep. I'm willing to bet he's there right now, pleased with himself. I have no doubt he killed that man."

"The undercover agent?"

"One of the men there said two men were new. So, it's a reasonable assumption that the agent is the dead guy. Call the sheriff."

She nodded and called the sheriff's office. The nighttime receptionist took her message with promises that someone would call her back as soon as possible.

By the time they reached the edge of town, Sheriff Westbrook called. Brynn put him on speaker so Weston could tell him about the dead man and keep both hands on the wheel.

"Are you insane?" The sheriff muttered something under his breath. "You deliberately put yourself in danger. Drury could have picked you off tonight."

"I wanted to bring him down before he could get to Brynn."

Brynn scowled at him. "We're in this together." She wanted to slap him.

"What you did was foolish," the sheriff said. "I'll alert Snowe so he can send someone out there. It most likely is the agent you found dead. You do something this reckless again, Hoover, and I'll lock you up for your own protection. We'll make sure the homeless community knows you didn't kill anyone." The sheriff hung up.

What he'd done had been foolish, but no more so than Brynn following him. How could she not have woken up when he stopped outside her door? His footsteps had probably set all of her senses on high alert.

"We need a better plan for catching Peter," she said once the sheriff hung up. "I don't want to be one of those girls in a horror movie who's too stupid to live. Tonight's actions were pretty stupid."

"Doing my best to keep you safe makes me stupid." He reached over and entwined his fingers with hers. "Yes, darlin', we're in this together. No more rushing off on my own. We'll let Peter come to us."

Good, because she'd do her darndest not to lose Weston. She gave his hand a squeeze as he pulled into her driveway.

Peter had said soon. His *soon* might not be her *soon* which would mean *now*, not days or weeks ahead. She shoved the door open, stepped out, and surveilled the area. Brynn was ready to face him now.

She followed Weston through the house making sure no one hid in the dark. All windows and doors were still locked. After all, Peter had been busy killing elsewhere.

Had it really been the death of his parents that sent him over the edge? She'd be upset, would mourn for a long time if something happened to her parents, but lose her mind? Murder? She didn't think so. The man had to have been insane long before they died.

Why her? According to Snowe, the man had money and a lot of it. Why obsess over a simple librarian from a small Ozark town? It made no sense.

House secure, and confident Weston wouldn't be making anymore late-night trips, at least that night, she undressed and crawled under the thick quilt. Fear of the mob had kept her heated for a bit, but after that, the cold seemed to have seeped into her bones.

From the room next door came the rustle of Weston undressing. A few minutes later, the flush of the bathroom toilet. How could she stay in this house after Peter was arrested and Weston moved back to his place?

Her parents had already said they wouldn't return, choosing the warmer climate of Florida after their travels. This little house would be lonely—something she'd never felt until she thought of Weston leaving.

She'd have to go back to work tomorrow, she thought as her eyes drifted closed. Later that day, actually. The library had been closed long enough. Brynn didn't have to worry about Peter. The Misty Angels would be by her side as usual.

The blaring of the alarm on her phone awoke her. Brynn peered at the clock. Six a.m. She'd gotten four hours of sleep. No, wait. The phone was ringing. She fumbled for it, dropping it to the floor. She reached down and saw her mother's face. Uh-oh. A video call. Picking up the phone, she pressed the button. "Hey, Mom."

Chapter Nineteen

"Why are you still in bed? I can hear it in your voice. Are you all right? We heard about the shooting at the diner. Someone said you had a stalker?" Her mother's voice rose with each question. "Your father and I are flying home. We'll be there in two days, maybe three."

Brynn squeezed her eyes shut. They'd be too late even if they could do something. "What happened at the diner was tragic, but it's over. The FBI know the identity of the shooter. There's no need for you two to fly home early."

"Your stalker?"

"More like a secret admirer. I have a friend staying with me. Seriously, everything is fine." She sure hoped she hadn't told her mother a lie. If they came home to attend her funeral, they'd never get over the loss of their only child. "Where are you now?"

"Morocco. It's quite lovely." Her mother sighed. "I really think we should come home."

"Don't be silly." Their being home would only give Peter more leverage over her.

"Why are you still in bed? Don't you have to go to work?"

"Yes, Mom. I was getting up when the phone rang." She sat up, hearing sounds of Weston getting ready. "I'll catch breakfast at the diner first."

"I'm going to worry about you every second until we return."

"Don't. Have a good time. I love you. Tell Dad the same."

"Love you, too, dear. If I find out you're lying to me, I'll be very upset. Your father says hello." Her mother hung up.

Brynn dressed quickly, opting for an easy ponytail to tame her hair, and hurried to the living room where Weston waited. "I hope my phone call didn't wake you."

"I was already awake." He smiled. "Sounded like you were getting scolded."

"These walls are too thin, and yes, I was on the verge of a severe tongue-lashing. Do your parents worry about you?" She shrugged into her coat.

"I lost them two years ago. One from cancer, the other from pneumonia."

He truly was alone in the world. "And then to lose your fiancée…" her heart ached for him.

"I'm okay." He gave her a one-armed hug. "Let's get this day started."

They rushed from the house to his truck. Brynn paused, her hand hovering near the door handle. "Where are the bikers?" The absence of their engines left the morning eerily quiet.

"Get in. I don't like this." Weston turned the key in the ignition.

An icy realization squeezed her heart. How could Peter prevent an entire group of tough men from arriving as scheduled? She checked her phone for local news of a fire. Where did the bikers live? As a group or in single-family homes? She knew little about them other than they were fierce protectors. "Something bad has happened."

"Don't invite trouble. We have enough as it is. The FBI just pulled in behind us. Maybe they told the bikers they were no longer needed since they now shadow us."

Relief flooded through her. "That makes sense." Especially since she hadn't found anything alarming in the local news.

They arrived at the diner before Lucy. Weston unlocked the back door and rushed Brynn inside. "Stay close." He flicked on lights as they headed down the short hall. Weston checked every room, including the freezer.

The tension she'd been holding in her shoulders eased to find the diner empty. "Just biscuits and gravy this morning."

"Chocolate or sausage?" Weston tied on his apron. "I've some chocolate and a couple of biscuits left over."

"Perfect." Brynn smiled and sat at a small table he'd moved into the kitchen to keep her from sitting in the eating area alone. She tried to read while she waited but couldn't concentrate on the words on the page.

What was Peter waiting for? What would he do when he apprehended her and Weston? Would he try to kill Weston right off? She gasped. What if he tortured him to coerce her to agree to whatever crazy demands he made?

"Stop." Weston glanced over. "I can tell you're freaking yourself out. We're being as vigilant as we can. There isn't much else we can do. Did you bring your pepper spray?"

"Yes. It's in my purse."

"Put it in your pocket." He turned back to the stove.

"Where's the gun?"

"Back of my waistband."

He was right. They were as prepared as they could be. She stood up and glanced out the window. The black SUV sat in the closest spot to the front door.

She stiffened. Without the bikers around, who would make sure she arrived at the library safely? Again, the thought that something had happened to them filled her mind. She'd grown fond of her guardian angels, especially Ron. *Lord, please don't let them be Peter's latest victims.*

Brynn watched Weston pour gravy on a plate of biscuits. "How can you be so calm all the time?"

"Who said I was calm?"

"You seem to be."

He set her breakfast in front of her. "I'm not sleeping well because of Peter. Wondering what his next move will be. But, I refuse to let it affect my daily life. Life is too short for that. I've learned that firsthand." His gaze settled on her. "Trust me, I'll do my best to keep you safe."

She cupped his face. "I know you will." She stood slightly to plant a light kiss on his lips. "You're my knight in shining armor."

He chuckled. "I'm not sure about that."

"One question, though. How am I getting to work?"

His eyes widened. "I'll ask the agents." He rushed off, returning a couple of minutes later. "The agent said they didn't tell the bikers not to come. They'll take you to the library now, and one of them will stay with you while the other two try to find out what happened to the Misty Angels."

~

Peter laughed. It had been so easy to slip inside the warehouse converted to living spaces. Now, all the bikers were in the common area stabbing him with looks that should have withered him on the spot. Instead, armed with his automatic rifle, he paced the floor in front of them.

"I would burn this building down with all of you in it, but concrete doesn't burn well. I could spray you all with bullets. That might be fun."

"What's your beef with us?" The one Peter figured was the leader crossed sinewy arms.

"You've made my job of reaching Brynlee more difficult. You shouldn't have been so cocky as to think I wouldn't find out where you lived. I'd have burned all your houses down if you'd been smart enough to have your own houses."

"No need. Ain't none of us married. What are you going to do to us?"

"Lock you in this room until I figure it out. I have big plans for this evening and don't have time to deal with you. But I need you out of the way."

"We'll hunt you down and kill you if you hurt our Brynlee. We already have a beef with you because you shot the sheriff. You killed that man at the homeless camp, too, right?"

Peter shrugged. "An undercover agent, incompetent at his job. I did the agency a service. Now, on the floor, backs together, hands behind you. I'm going to make you very cozy. Don't cooperate, and you all die. Come on. Time is a wastin'." He aimed the weapon at them.

They did exactly as instructed, and he tied them with vinyl rope. He should kill them, but he didn't feel like it. All he needed was for them to stay out of his way long enough for him to nab Brynlee and flee.

The bikers would find a way out of the rope, but not for a good while. "There we go. Good evening, Gentlemen." Peter closed the door after him and stuck a broom handle through the handles of the door.

Behind the building waited the van he'd stolen from a local plumber. No one would think twice about seeing the vehicle on the road, and the plumber wouldn't miss the van until morning. Peter had thought of every tiny detail. Even how to get to the chef and Brynlee.

He turned off the van lights before approaching the diner and pulled behind the building to keep out of sight of the SUV out front. He'd made a key to the back door days before when he'd snuck into Brynlee's house and 'borrowed' the chef's keys.

Armed with his rifle, he unlocked the door and stepped inside.

~

Weston carried a stack of trays to the storage room. He froze as the back door opened and he found himself staring down the barrel of an automatic rifle. "Hello, Peter."

"If you say it louder, Brynlee might hear and run. We don't want that. Back to the kitchen, Chef."

Weston backed up the way he had come, not wanting to turn his back on Peter. He mouthed that he was sorry when Brynn caught a glimpse of the man behind him.

Lucy gasped.

"Hold in that scream, ma'am. Wouldn't want you to alert the feds. Why don't you step into that freezer over there. Someone will find you in time."

Lucy paled and did as she was told. At least the man didn't plan on killing her. "Now what?" Weston set the trays on the counter.

"The three of us head quietly out the back. You're expendable, Chef. I'll kill you where you stand if you don't comply. Hands up. Brynlee, please remove the gun from the back of his waistband. I can see that he has one."

She nodded and retrieved the gun.

"Now, set it on the counter and back away."

She glanced up at Weston and obeyed.

"Now, put your hands up. Chef, lead the way."

Weston released a heavy sigh and headed for the back door.

"Open it with one hand, keeping the other up."

He gritted his teeth and complied. Without his coat, the frigid air bit straight to the bone.

Peter stepped around them and opened the back door to a white van with a plumber's logo on the side. "Stand in front of the door, hands behind you." He secured their hands with zip ties. "Now get in."

Climbing into the van with his hands bound wasn't too difficult, but Brynn's shorter legs needed help. She pulled back when Peter reached out to help her.

He frowned and grasped her arm. "Either I help you, or I toss you in. Your choice."

Her lips curled, but she let him help her up. He

closed the door, plunging them into darkness.

"Weston?" Brynn's whisper.

"Over here." He put his back against a toolbox and lowered to the floor. "Follow my voice."

She shrieked as the van started.

Weston grunted as she fell on top of him. "Are you all right?"

"Yes. You broke my fall." She maneuvered until she sat next to him. "I can't believe he simply waltzed into the diner. The man is like a ghost."

"Not anymore. We know exactly where he is." The FBI agents should've been inside the diner, not outside in their vehicle.

"You aren't wearing the shirt with the button that has the tracker on it, are you?"

"Nope. The sheriff can track our phones as long as they're on, but I don't think Peter is stupid enough to let me keep my phone."

"Mine is in my purse at the diner. But, I have the pepper spray in my pocket."

"Lot of good that does with your hands tied." He'd find a way out of their predicament. All he had to do was keep his wits about him. Weston grimaced as he leaned his head against the toolbox. Well, he'd failed again at keeping Brynn safe. What made him think he could keep her alive?

"I watched a video once on how to get out of zip ties. I'm wearing gym shoes, so it should work."

"Can you get your hands in front of you?"

"Yes, but it will take a bit of maneuvering and some time. Once I'm free, I'm sure I can find something here to cut yours." She bumped against him as she struggled to bring her arms in front of her.

"There isn't much space."

"We're slowing down." Their freedom would have to wait. Hopefully, Peter wouldn't kill him right off.

The light of a full moon pierced his eyes when Peter opened the back doors. Weston scooted out first. In front of them was an abandoned farmhouse with boarded-up windows. It promised to be a very cold night.

"It ain't much, folks, but it's been home the last couple of nights. There are blankets inside." Peter motioned them ahead of him. "I should've grabbed some food from the diner. I haven't had an opportunity to do much shopping because of my face being plastered all over the news."

He opened the front door. "I've got a room for you, Chef, while I have a little chat with Brynlee."

He locked Weston in the bathroom. Weston did the only thing he could do—he leaned his forehead against the door and prayed.

Chapter Twenty

Brynn kept a wary eye on Peter as he followed her to the living room. She sat next to a pile of blankets on the floor. "Would you mind draping one of these around my shoulders? I'm freezing."

He propped the gun against the wall and covered her with a wool blanket. He set a cell phone the floor and smashed it with his foot. "Are you a cold-weather or warm-weather person?"

"I like all the seasons. Why?" The blanket helped a little against the cold.

"It will let me know whether to head north or south with you." He sat cross-legged in front of her and lit a propane lantern which gave off a little heat. "I'm thinking Mexico myself. I'm over the bitter winters." He tilted his head and stared at her. "Even not dolled up for a party, you're beautiful."

She wanted to gag. "Why me?"

"When I saw you across the room at the Christmas party and you smiled, it hit me like a lightning bolt. You belong with me."

"I don't know you, Peter." She shivered from more than the cold.

"You will soon enough. You'll grow to love me, as

I do you." He smiled. "I've enough money to give you a life of luxury."

She doubted that. Surely, his accounts had been frozen by now. If not, they would be once the authorities realized she and Weston had been kidnapped.

"What are you doing to do with Weston?"

"Kill him." His brow furrowed. "Surely, you realize you can't have both of us?"

"He and I are only friends."

"Right." He snorted. "I'm not a fool. With him out of the picture, you'll have just me."

The man truly was insane. At a loss for words, she simply stared at him. Most people would squirm under such scrutiny, but Peter seemed to find it amusing.

"You should get some sleep." He took a blanket from the pile and rolled up in it.

The last thing she wanted was sleep. She worked on trying to free herself until exhaustion won out. The zip ties were so tight they bit into her skin, cutting off her circulation. Using the pile of blankets as a pillow, she fell asleep.

Brynn woke to find Peter gone. She struggled awkwardly to her feet and peered out a hole in the wood covering one of the windows. No sign of the van. She studied the room the best she could through the dimness for something to help her free her hands, then wandered in the direction Weston had been taken. "Weston?"

"The bathroom. Are you free?"

"Not yet. It's harder than it looked on the video. Peter has gone somewhere."

Something crashed on the other side of the door.

"What was that?"

"I dropped the lid to the toilet tank. I'm trying to get a sharp edge to cut through these ties."

Smart. "I'll keep trying on my end. I hear the van." She quickly returned to where she'd slept and pretended like Peter woke her when he entered the house.

"I've brought breakfast." He set a fast-food egg and sausage sandwich in front of her. "Guess the van hasn't been reported stolen yet."

"What about Weston?"

"Dead men don't need to eat." He unwrapped the sandwich and held it to her mouth. "But women who want to live do."

She forced herself to allow him to feed her. When she'd finished, he held a plastic cup with a straw to her lips. A diet soda.

"I know this isn't what you're used to eating. Unfortunately, the world will miss Hoover's cooking. The man is a very good chef. Too good for this town. He should've stayed in the big city."

If he had, he wouldn't be in this trouble with her. As much as she wished he wasn't, she couldn't imagine going through it all alone.

"I'm not forcing you, Brynlee." Peter tilted his head again. "You do have a choice whether to be with me or not."

"If I say no?"

"Then, I kill you along with your friend. You have until nightfall to give me your decision. Perhaps, by then, you'll know me well enough to say yes."

Oh, she knew him well enough. If she said yes, it would only be to save Weston's life. "What do you want me to know?"

"That I have bank accounts the authorities can't seize. More money than you'll see in your lifetime. Homes in other countries. A private jet. I've put all that on hold to pursue you."

"Couldn't you have found a woman from your social circle?"

"I did. Once. Unfortunately, I caught her cheating, and she is no longer with us. The pain of that brought me here to Misty Hollow. I liked the appearance of the new hotel when I saw it online and came to see it in person. It, as well as Hoover, are out of place in this town." He wrapped a blanket around her. "You should stop trying to break the ties. Your wrists are starting to bleed. I don't have any first-aid supplies here." He spoke to her in a detached voice, not as a man who loved a woman. More like he'd decided to take her and couldn't veer from that path. "I did enjoy our little game with the book, but then it became time to do things my way. The book took too long."

"I hated the game. You took one of my favorite books and ruined it for me." She squirmed against the pain in her back from sitting on the cold floor.

"Not at all." He looked confused. "It's something we can share. Imagine the story of how we met when our future children ask."

"I don't think I would tell anyone you killed people in order to marry me."

"Maybe not." He cleared his throat. "People would frown on that, wouldn't they? But money, my dear, buys respect. No one would dare say anything to our faces."

Why wouldn't he leave? She needed her arms in front of her so she could reach her pocket. "I can't feel my arms." If she could get him to free her, she could go for the pepper spray.

"I cannot untie you."

"Why not? Where am I going to go? I wouldn't think of running and leaving Weston behind."

"You still think too highly of him." His voice hardened. "But, you're right. You wouldn't leave him behind. Turn around."

Her heartbeat increased as he cut the ties.

"Let me see your hands." He clicked his tongue at the sight of where the plastic had cut into her skin. "I'll use some of the bottled water to clean them." He reached for the corner of one of the blankets.

Brynn plunged her hand into her pocket and pulled out the pepper spray. She pressed the button and aimed for his eyes, averting her face.

He howled and covered his face.

Taking opportunity, she bolted down the hall toward the bathroom and unlocked the door. Who had put the lock on backward? Peter? No one else would want to lock someone in rather than out. She opened it in time to see Weston's face.

Bullets peppered the ceiling above her head. Plaster rained on her hair. Brynn screamed and ducked, then turned toward her stalker.

"So, you've made your choice." Peter, eyes streaming, held the rifle in his hands. "Which of you should I kill first? Or...I have an idea." An evil grin spread across his face. "Back inside the bathroom, Chef. Brynlee, lock the door. We've another game to play."

Heart in her throat, her gaze locked with Weston's as she locked him in again. She turned to Peter. "What kind of game?"

"I'm going to tie you up. A contest of sorts. You'll have a certain amount of time to free yourself, or both of you will die."

"Where are you going to be?"

"I'm going to go kill your angel friends." He shook his head. "Don't be angry with me, sweetheart. This is all because of your choice. Then, if you free yourself, I'll hunt you down and kill you. In fact, I'll hunt you for the rest of your life." He motioned the gun back to the living room.

Using nylon rope, he tied her hands together, then wound the rope around her ankles. "You'll manage to escape, but not until this house is burning real hot." He tugged the rope, then kissed the top of her head. "We could've had a good life together, Brynlee."

God help her.

Peter poured a thin line of gasoline along the walls. Then, he unlocked the bathroom door. Sounds of a scuffle, then a thud, almost stopped her heart.

"What did you do to him?" She screamed as he struck a match and tossed it near the front door.

"Made things a little more difficult is all. *Adios.*" He gave a little salute and dashed out the door.

Brynn wasted no time. She tugged on the rope until the pain in her wrists became too great, then she started chewing. Fibers stuck to her tongue. She spit and kept going.

Already the heat from the flames banished the winter chill from the room. The blankets next to her smoldered, and she scooted to the center of the room. "Weston!"

The rope fibers cut her lip. The metallic taste of

blood filled her mouth. The door Peter had left open taunted her. The air coming from outside was the only thing that kept her from choking, both from fear and the smoke.

She wasn't going to free herself in time to save them. "Weston!" Sobs racked her body. Tears streamed down her cheeks, soaking the rope in her mouth.

~

Weston groaned and put a hand to his forehead, bringing it away sticky with blood. Peter had knocked him hard with the butt of the gun. He sniffed, then coughed. His nightmare had come true. He and Brynn were in a burning building.

He crawled from the bathroom, surprised to see the front door open. What kind of game was Peter playing?

Brynn called out his name. He staggered to his feet as flames licked at the walls on either side of him. The accelerant Peter had used left spots on the stained fabric. He stumbled into the living room.

"Here." He fell to his knees beside her and untied her. Not an easy task with the shredded rope, but he managed. "We need to get out of here."

"You're bleeding."

"So are you. Stay low. We'll have to run through the flames." His heart constricted. "Can you?"

"It's better than burning to death in here." She gripped his hand.

Bent at the waist, they raced for the door, jumping over the flames between them and freedom. Brynn squealed and beat at the flame eating at the hem of her pants.

Weston beat the small flame out with his hands, then pulled her away from the house. The van that had brought them there was gone. "I have no idea which way is town. We'll follow this poor excuse for a road." They weren't out of danger yet. They'd freeze before they reached town.

"We're on the mountain." Brynn wrapped her arms around herself. "This will lead to the main road. Hopefully, someone will give us a ride."

He prayed it wouldn't be another infatuated psycho. "Why didn't Peter kill us?" He pulled her close as they walked.

"Because he intends to stalk me for the rest of my life. If we escaped the house."

No need to ask how the man would know. Their abduction and escape would make all the newspapers. He shivered so violently, his teeth chattered. "Doesn't it feel like déjà vu?"

She gave a nervous giggle. "Sure does. Let's hope it has a better ending."

"Hold up." He went to the side of the road and retched. "Sorry. Peter hit me hard. I'm pretty sure I have a concussion."

"Can you make it?"

"Yep."

"I don't think he expected you to wake up. He wanted me to have to choose between saving myself or saving you." She wrapped her arms around his waist. "I'm so glad I didn't have to make that choice." Brynn peered up at him. "I love you, Weston Hoover."

He smiled. "I love you, Brynlee Bourge, but I'm not going to kiss you until I have a chance to brush my teeth."

She laughed and hugged him harder. "Then we'd better hurry home."

By the time they reached the main road, he couldn't feel his feet. "Look." He turned Brynn's attention to the white van surrounded by bikers and Peter lying on the ground.

"Howdy." Ron grinned and approached them. "We have some coats for you. Here's the keys to the van."

"How did you find us?" Weston took the keys.

"Figured he brought you up here somewhere. The fire told us where. When we reached the place, we spotted the van the owner reported stolen." He motioned for one of his men to bring them coats. "This scoundrel had us tied up, or we'd have been here sooner. Deputy Hudson came to see why we didn't pick up Miss Brynlee and cut us loose."

Weston helped Brynn with her coat, then donned his. The coat smelled of cigarettes and beer, but provided much-needed warmth. "You're a lifesaver. Thanks." He led Brynn to the van. "Let's crank this heater on high and go home."

"Is it home to you?" Her voice shook.

"Of course, it is. Did you think I'd leave once the danger was over? I could never walk away from you, Brynn.

"Good." She smiled.

Once Peter, trussed like a holiday turkey, had been placed in the back of the van, Weston drove to the sheriff's office. "I've never been happier to take out the garbage."

~

Reluctant to let Weston out of her sight, she curled up with him on the sofa under a thick quilt. She moved a wet strand of hair off his forehead. "You can't go to sleep for a while yet. Not with that bump on your head."

"What do you suggest we do to fill our time?" He wiggled his eyebrows.

"I think you should kiss me." She lifted her face and closed her eyes.

"Open your eyes, Brynn." He cupped her face.

"Okay." She peered into his eyes.

"Marry me. Let's get married as soon as we can."

"Really?" Joy bubbled through her like Champagne.

"Yes. Despite this crazy winter with Peter, I like the town and the people. One woman stands out as my favorite. I know it's probably not wise to form a relationship under such cir—"

"Shut up and kiss me, or I'll say no." She didn't think her smile could get any wider.

He pulled her onto his lap, tangled his hands in her hair, and kissed her. Long, hard, and heated. Her arms wrapped around his neck.

The clearing of a throat made her look up.

"Hi, Mom and Dad. Meet Weston, the man I'm going to marry."

Mom arched a brow. "I certainly hope so after that display of affection."

Brynn slid reluctantly from Weston's lap. "Dad, can you look at Weston's head? He has quite the lump." She glanced back at Weston. "He's a doctor."

"So, you're going to marry my daughter, huh?" He peered into Weston's eyes.

"Yes, sir. As soon as possible."

"Guess we shortened our trip just in time." Dad smiled. "You'll live. Nasty concussion, so you'll have a headache for a few days, but nothing time won't heal."

"Would you mind going into the kitchen with your wife?" Weston smiled at Brynn. "You interrupted something."

Her father laughed. "Sure thing. We'll make coffee, then the two of you can let us in on what we've only heard bits and pieces of."

Alone again, Weston pulled Brynn back on his lap and picked up where they'd left off.

The End

Dear Reader,

I truly hope you enjoyed Brynn's and Weston's story. If so, please leave a review on Amazon. Have you read the other Misty Hollow romantic suspenses? You can find the links below. You're sure to enjoy them as you see how a small, secluded town deals with danger and romance with strong heroes and heroines. Join in the adventures and read them all.

God bless!

www.cynthiahickey.com

Cynthia Hickey is a multi-published and best-selling author of cozy mysteries and romantic suspense. She has taught writing at many conferences and small writing retreats. She and her husband run the publishing press, Winged Publications, which includes some of the CBA's best well-known authors. They live in Arizona and Arkansas, becoming snowbirds with two dogs and one cat. They have ten grandchildren who keep them busy and tell everyone they know that "Nana is a writer."

Connect with me on FaceBook
Twitter
Sign up for my newsletter and receive a free short story

www.cynthiahickey.com

Follow me on Amazon
And Bookbub

Enjoy other books by Cynthia Hickey

Misty Hollow
Secrets of Misty Hollow
Deceptive Peace
Calm Surface
Lightning Never Strikes Twice
Lethal Inheritance
Bitter Isolation
Say I Don't
Christmas Stalker

Stay in Misty Hollow for a while. Get the entire series here!

The Tail Waggin' Mysteries
Cat-Eyed Witness
The Dog Who Found a Body
Troublesome Twosome
Four-Legged Suspect
Unwanted Christmas Guest

Wedding Day Cat Burglar

Brothers Steele
Sharp as Steele
Carved in Steele
Forged in Steele
Brothers Steele (All three in one)

The Brothers of Copper Pass
Wyatt's Warrant
Dirk's Defense
Stetson's Secret
Houston's Hope
Dallas's Dare
Seth's Sacrifice
Malcolm's Misunderstanding
The Brothers of Copper Pass Boxed Set

Time Travel
The Portal

Tiny House Mysteries
No Small Caper
Caper Goes Missing
Caper Finds a Clue
Caper's Dark Adventure
A Strange Game for Caper
Caper Steals Christmas
Caper Finds a Treasure
Tiny House Mysteries boxed set

Wife for Hire – Private Investigators
Saving Sarah
Lesson for Lacey
Mission for Meghan
Long Way for Lainie
Aimed at Amy
Wife for Hire (all five in one)

A Hollywood Murder
Killer Pose, book 1
Killer Snapshot, book 2
Shoot to Kill, book 3
Kodak Kill Shot, book 4
To Snap a Killer
Hollywood Murder Mysteries

Shady Acres Mysteries
Beware the Orchids, book 1
Path to Nowhere
Poison Foliage
Poinsettia Madness
Deadly Greenhouse Gases
Vine Entrapment
Shady Acres Boxed Set

CLEAN BUT GRITTY Romantic Suspense

Highland Springs

Murder Live
Say Bye to Mommy
To Breathe Again

Highland Springs Murders (all 3 in one)

Colors of Evil Series

Shades of Crimson
Coral Shadows

The Pretty Must Die Series

Ripped in Red, book 1
Pierced in Pink, book 2
Wounded in White, book 3
Worthy, The Complete Story

Lisa Paxton Mystery Series

Eenie Meenie Miny Mo
Jack Be Nimble
Hickory Dickory Dock
Boxed Set

Hearts of Courage
A Heart of Valor
The Game
Suspicious Minds
After the Storm
Local Betrayal
Hearts of Courage Boxed Set

Overcoming Evil series
Mistaken Assassin
Captured Innocence

CHRISTMAS STALKER

Mountain of Fear
Exposure at Sea
A Secret to Die for
Collision Course
Romantic Suspense of 5 books in 1

INSPIRATIONAL

Nosy Neighbor Series
Anything For A Mystery, Book 1
A Killer Plot, Book 2
Skin Care Can Be Murder, Book 3
Death By Baking, Book 4
Jogging Is Bad For Your Health, Book 5
Poison Bubbles, Book 6
A Good Party Can Kill You, Book 7
Nosy Neighbor collection

Christmas with Stormi Nelson

The Summer Meadows Series
Fudge-Laced Felonies, Book 1
Candy-Coated Secrets, Book 2
Chocolate-Covered Crime, Book 3
Maui Macadamia Madness, Book 4
All four novels in one collection

The River Valley Mystery Series
Deadly Neighbors, Book 1
Advance Notice, Book 2
The Librarian's Last Chapter, Book 3

All three novels in one collection

Historical cozy
Hazel's Quest

Historical Romances
Runaway Sue
Taming the Sheriff
Sweet Apple Blossom
A Doctor's Agreement
A Lady Maid's Honor
A Touch of Sugar
Love Over Par
Heart of the Emerald
A Sketch of Gold
Her Lonely Heart

Finding Love the Harvey Girl Way
Cooking With Love
Guiding With Love
Serving With Love
Warring With Love
All 4 in 1

Finding Love in Disaster
The Rancher's Dilemma
The Teacher's Rescue
The Soldier's Redemption

CHRISTMAS STALKER

Woman of courage Series

A Love For Delicious
Ruth's Redemption
Charity's Gold Rush
Mountain Redemption
They Call Her Mrs. Sheriff
Woman of Courage series

Short Story Westerns
Desert Rose
Desert Lilly
Desert Belle
Desert Daisy
Flowers of the Desert 4 in 1

Contemporary

Romance in Paradise
Maui Magic
Sunset Kisses
Deep Sea Love
3 in 1

Finding a Way Home
Service of Love
Hillbilly Cinderella
Unraveling Love
I'd Rather Kiss My Horse

Christmas
Dear Jillian

Romancing the Fabulous Cooper Brothers
Handcarved Christmas
The Payback Bride
Curtain Calls and Christmas Wishes
Christmas Gold
A Christmas Stamp
Snowflake Kisses
Merry's Secret Santa
A Christmas Deception

The Red Hat's Club (Contemporary novellas)

Finally
Suddenly
Surprisingly
The Red Hat's Club 3 – in 1

Short Story

One Hour (A short story thriller)
Whisper Sweet Nothings (a Valentine short romance)

Made in the USA
Las Vegas, NV
20 August 2023